Ann Coburn has written extensively for the stage and TV and is the author of several novels for older children, including *Glint*, which won an Arts Council Writer's Award and a Northern Writer's Award, and The Borderlands Sequence, a quartet of novels that also won an Arts Council Writer's Award. Before becoming a full-time writer, Ann worked as an English teacher in an inner-city comprehensive school. She has given talks and run creative writing workshops for children and adults since her first novel was published in 1991. Ann lives in Northumberland.

You can find out more about Ann and her books by visiting her w

Books by the same author

Dream Team Mission 1:
Flying Solo

Dream Team Mission 2:
Showtime

Dream Team Mission 4:
The Daydream Shift

Mission 3: Speed Challenge

Ann Coburn

For Isabella Kate, with love.
May all your dreams be delivered.

First published 2007 by Walker Books Ltd
87 Vauxhall Walk, London SE11 5HJ

2 4 6 8 10 9 7 5 3 1

This book has been typeset in Stone Informal

Printed and bound in Great Britain by Creative Print and Design (Wales), Ebbw Vale

British Library Cataloguing in Publication Data:
a catalogue record for this book is available
from the British Library

ISBN 978-1-84428-072-8

www.walkerbooks.co.uk

Contents

Trouble

Trouble arrived with the morning post. Snaffle was eating his breakfast in the Mess Hall and trying to ignore the automated mailskoot as it zipped from table to table. The little machine was almost hidden under a particularly large postbag. It was the day of the speed challenge and just about every trainee

Dream Fetcher in the Dream Centre had been sent Good Luck or Thinking of You cards.

Snaffle scowled. He would not be getting a card from his family. His parents did not believe in luck. His older brother Grabble had been the top trainee in his year and now he, Snaffle, was expected to do just as well. He scowled even harder and stabbed his spoon into his bowl of hot Dream Waffles. His parents were in for a big disappointment. He was not the top trainee in his dream centre. He did not even hold the top place in his own measly dream team. Halfway through training he was sharing bottom place with Midge. Harley was second, and Vert – timid Vert! – was first.

A familiar mixture of rage and bewilderment began to burn in Snaffle as he scowled at Midge, Vert and Harley. How could he be in bottom place when the other members of his dream team were such losers? The way they dressed said it all. Midge was swamped by her uniform. Dream Fetchers were supposed to be at least seven centimetres tall, and she had stopped growing at six and three quarters – so even the smallest standard-issue uniform was too big for her. Her sleeves had the biggest turn-ups Snaffle had ever seen and her helmet was so loose, it wobbled when she walked.

Vert had the opposite problem. His faded, second-hand uniform was far too

tight, especially around the stomach. Harley's uniform was at least a good fit, but her jacket was stained with oil and smeared with dreamskoot engine grease. Added to that, Harley always wore a raggedy old kerchief, tied cowboy-style around her neck. It was against regulations to wear anything that was not part of the uniform. Harley got away with it because the kerchief had once belonged to her mother, who had died fighting in the Battle of the Gateway.

Snaffle checked out his reflection in the shiny metal surface of a large tea urn. He was pleased with what he saw. His uniform had been made by the best tailor in Dreamside. It fitted perfectly and the added shoulder pads made his chest look broader. Snaffle straightened his back, pushed a stray lock of hair into place and gave a satisfied smirk.

"Looking good, Snaffle!" said Harley from across the table.

Snaffle stopped smirking. Had Harley seen him admiring his reflection? Quickly he shifted his gaze away from the tea urn and pretended to be studying the Mess Hall noticeboard.

"You look ever so smart this morning," continued Harley.

Snaffle scowled. He did not trust praise. His brother Grabble always followed it up with something nasty. Snaffle glared across at Harley, waiting for her to do the same, but Harley just smiled at him. Before he could stop himself, Snaffle smiled back. What was happening to him? Soon they would all be rivals as they each tried to complete the speed challenge in the fastest time. He should not be sharing smiles with Harley! He tried to find his scowl again but could not quite manage it. The trouble was, he was becoming fond of his Dream Team mates.

"Snaffle always looks smart. Not like the rest of us," giggled Midge.

"Excuse me?" said Harley, smoothing down her oil-stained jacket and pretending to be hurt. "Did you hear that, Vert? Midge doesn't think we look smart."

They all turned to look at Vert. He was clutching his usual mission-morning breakfast – a glass of hot water – and staring miserably into the rising steam. He was very pale and the points of his ears were drooping badly.

"Poor Vert," said Midge, reaching across the table and squeezing his hand. "Nerves again?"

Vert nodded and managed a wobbly smile.

"I don't know what he's got to be nervous about," grumbled Snaffle. "He's in the lead!"

"Yeah, Vert, I don't get it," said Harley. "You're in top place after our first two

missions. Doesn't that make you less nervous?"

Vert shook his head.

"Don't worry," soothed Midge. "Once you're flying, you'll forget all about those silly nerves."

At the mention of flying, Vert whimpered and turned a delicate shade of green. Only Snaffle noticed. He narrowed his eyes and began to watch Vert very carefully.

"Yeah, you'll be too busy enjoying yourself," said Harley, her eyes shining with excitement. "Who wouldn't? Especially the speed challenge! Just think – we're allowed to fly our dreamskoots as fast as we want. Zoom!"

Vert gulped and put a hand over his mouth. Again, only Snaffle noticed. Midge and Harley had moved on to swapping tips for faster Earthside flying. The more they talked of dreamskoot flips, speed cornering and backward loops, the more Vert looked horrified. Snaffle frowned. What was his problem?

Harley was in the middle of telling Vert how to do a rooftop skid when she was interrupted by squeals of delight from the dream team at the next table. The mailskoot had zipped up and placed a large sunshine-yellow cone in front of a blushing trainee.

"Oh, look!" cried Midge. "A Luck Shower!"

Harley turned to watch the action, leaving Vert free to slump back in his chair with a sigh of relief. The trainee at the next table took a firm grip on a tail of string coming from the bottom of her Luck Shower. Her team mates began a countdown.

"Five! Four! Three! Two! One..."

The trainee yanked on the string and the top of the cone opened up like a daisy. With a chorus of whizzes, whistles and pops, a mass of bright spirals exploded from the cone.

They shot up almost to the ceiling of the Mess Hall before they ran out of energy and floated slowly downwards, twisting and turning in the air.

The trainee and her team mates tilted back their heads, opened their mouths and tried to catch as many of the little spirals as they could. Midge and Harley did the same, snapping up the spirals that floated over their table. The little mailskoot folded its mechanical arms and hovered in place, humming impatiently as it waited for the Luck Shower to finish.

"Yum! Chocolate," laughed Harley, licking her lips. She caught another spiral. "And that one was candyfloss."

"Strawberries and cream," giggled Midge as a spiral melted on her tongue.

"Come on, Snaffle!" said Harley. "It's supposed to be lucky to catch one."

"So childish," muttered Snaffle, refusing to join in.

"Whatever," grinned Harley. She turned to Vert. "Go on! See if you can get lucky."

Vert glanced up at the swirling luck spirals and turned paper white. He closed his eyes, grabbed the edge of the table with both hands and held on tight.

"Aha!" said Snaffle triumphantly, glancing between the tumbling spirals and Vert's white knuckles. "I see!"

Midge and Harley both stopped

catching spirals and looked at Snaffle.

"What do you see?" asked Midge.

"I see why Vert is so nervous before a mission," said Snaffle.

"Why?" asked Harley.

"He's scared of flying."

Midge and Harley both laughed. A Dream Fetcher afraid of flying? That was just stupid.

"He is!" insisted Snaffle. "He can't even look at those flying spirals without feeling sick."

Midge and Harley looked at their team mate properly for the first time that morning.

"Oh," breathed Harley, seeing the fear in Vert's eyes.

"Is Snaffle right?" whispered Midge.

Vert nodded miserably. A shocked silence fell. They sat without moving as the remains of the Luck Shower drifted down around them, settling softly on the table top and floor.

Beside them the mailskoot gave a wheezy sigh, pulled out a dustpan and brush, and swept up the fallen luck spirals. Then it scanned the number on the end of their table, pulled a small pile of envelopes from the postbag and dumped them next to the teapot.

"But why?" asked Midge once the mailskoot had zipped off to the next table. "Why are you training to be a

Dream Fetcher when you're – well, you know –"

"Scared of flying," said Snaffle with a smirk. "Really, really scared. Terrified, by the looks of it."

"It does seem a bit odd, Vert," said Harley, sending Snaffle a withering look. "I mean, flying is what a Dream Fetcher does."

"No, it isn't," corrected Midge. "Delivering dreams is what a Dream Fetcher does."

"Whatever," said Harley, who privately considered dream delivery to be an annoying interruption to a good flight. "The point is, a Dream Fetcher has to spend a lot of time up in the air. And you're, you know –"

"Scared of flying," Snaffle finished promptly. He was beginning to enjoy himself. "Very, very scared. So scared, he can't even stuff his face the way he does every other mor— Ow!" Snaffle came to a sudden stop and glared around the table. Someone had just kicked him.

"Why, Vert?" Midge asked softly.

For answer, Vert picked an envelope from the pile of post on the table and handed it to Midge to open. "Read it out," he said.

Midge pulled a large Good Luck card from the envelope. *"To our dear Vert,"* she read. *"The first one in our family to make it as a Dream Fetcher. We are so proud of you, son. Love, Mum and Dad."*

"That's why," said Vert with a wry

smile. "How can I tell them I'd rather be a Dream Chef? They've been saving up to pay for my Dream Fetcher training ever since I was born."

Snaffle blinked. What a surprise. He and Vert had something in common. They were both trying to keep their parents happy. For the first time he began to feel a bit sorry for his team mate.

"Oh, Vert!" said Midge.

"Don't. Don't worry about me. I've muddled through so far, haven't I?"

"But there must be something we can do to help."

"Just don't tell Team Leader Flint," Vert begged. "Please?"

"Wouldn't dream of it," said Harley. "Would we, Snaffle?"

Snaffle looked sideways at Harley. After their last mission, when he had tried to bring down Vert's score by telling tales, Harley had made him promise to play fair for the rest of their training.

"We wouldn't tell. Would we, Snaffle?" Harley insisted.

Snaffle scowled at her. "No," he sighed. "We wouldn't."

"Because we're a dream team. That means we're family, right?"

"Right," Snaffle muttered.

Harley beamed at him. Snaffle tried to

sneer but his heart wasn't in it. The truth was, he rather liked the idea of winning the speed challenge fair and square. He began to size up his team mates. He knew he could beat Midge and Vert. Midge was too curious about humans to ever make a clean, quick dream delivery. As for Vert, he was possibly the slowest dreamskoot rider in the whole of Dreamside. Harley was a different matter. She could handle her dreamskoot very well. Snaffle knew he would have to be on top form to beat her. While the other three opened their post, he sat back and imagined how good it would feel to be the first one home.

"Hey, Snaffle!" Harley yelled.

Snaffle jumped. His daydream about winning the speed challenge popped like a balloon. He glared at Harley. "What?" he growled.

"I said, aren't you going to open your post?" said Harley, holding out a thick cream-coloured envelope.

Snaffle felt his heart give a little leap of joy. The envelope bore the official seal of the dream centre where his father was Area Commander. His family had sent him a Good Luck card after all! He grabbed the envelope. It crackled stiffly in his hands as he turned it over. Carefully, he broke the seal, opened the flap and pulled out a folded sheet of paper.

"It's a proper letter," he said smugly. "That's much better than a card."

As Snaffle settled down to read his

letter, Midge shared a delighted smile with Harley and Vert. It had been no fun opening their post on mission mornings while Snaffle sat empty-handed, pretending he didn't care. Everyone deserved at least one Good Luck wish on mission mornings – even Snaffle.

"Go on, then," said Midge after a moment. "What does it say?"

Snaffle did not answer. He was still staring down at the letter.

"Is everything OK?" Vert asked.

"Everything's great!" said Snaffle, scrunching up the sheet of paper and dropping it into the teapot. "Smashing!" he added, sending his bowl of Dream Waffles skidding across the table to Vert. "There you go!" he said, giving Vert a smile like a box full of knives. "Tuck in! You can't do the speed challenge on an empty stomach."

Vert took one look at the soggy waffles and slammed both hands over his mouth.

"Hey!" said Midge, pushing the bowl back to Snaffle. "That wasn't very nice!"

"Nice doesn't work," said Snaffle, standing up and kicking his chair away. "Not if you want to be the best."

"Snaffle," Harley warned. "Remember your promise."

Snaffle showed her his new smile that was not really a smile at all. "What promise?" he said, and then he turned his back and walked away from his dream team.

Velvet

As soon as Snaffle was out of sight, Midge fished his crumpled letter from the teapot. The paper was soggy, the ink had run and most of the words had turned into unreadable splodges. Midge smoothed out the paper and even more ink smudged away under her hand. She frowned down at the letter, trying to make sense of the few remaining words.

"What does it say?" Vert asked.

"Um. Something about Snaffle's low points score and an imp."

"An imp?" said Harley. "Why are they writing about an imp?"

"No, hang on. Not imp. Improve. It says, *You must improve your points score whatever it takes.* Then that line there says, *You are a family ...*"

"A family what?" Harley asked.

"I'm not sure. The next word is smudged but it begins with a 'D'."

"Family delight?" guessed Vert.

"Family darling?" suggested Harley.

Midge peered at the smudged word again, picking out letters. "Oh dear," she sighed. "No wonder Snaffle was upset. It says, *You are a family disgrace.*" She screwed up the letter and jumped to her feet. "We have to stop him before he tells Team Leader Flint about Vert."

"But he promised he wouldn't," protested Vert as Harley hustled him out of his chair.

"That was before the letter," said Midge, grabbing her helmet. "Right now, Snaffle would do anything for extra points."

"But would Team Leader Flint give him points for telling tales?" asked Harley.

"I'm not waiting to find out," said Midge, beginning to run.

Together they raced out of the Mess Hall and skidded around the corner just as the doors at the other end of the corridor sighed shut behind Snaffle.

"Come on!" Harley yelled. "We can still catch him!"

They sprinted down the corridor and pushed through the doors into the noise and bustle of the Dream Centre. It was a vast and busy place, split into two very different halves. The half they were standing in was full of staff hurrying between the workplaces along the back wall. First in line was the Switchboard Room, where all incoming dream orders were logged and sorted. Next door were the Dream Kitchens, where teams of chefs worked around the clock to prepare and bake the dreams ready for delivery. The dreamskoot garages and repair shops were at the far end of the row and, in the roof space high above, the Dream Traffic Control Tower looked out over the whole of the Dream Centre.

Midge, Harley and Vert came to a halt and searched the crowds for any sign of Snaffle or Team Leader Flint. Midge stood on her tiptoes to get a better view.

"E-excuse me..?" piped a little voice, right beside her.

Midge nearly dropped her helmet. She turned towards the voice with a scowl.

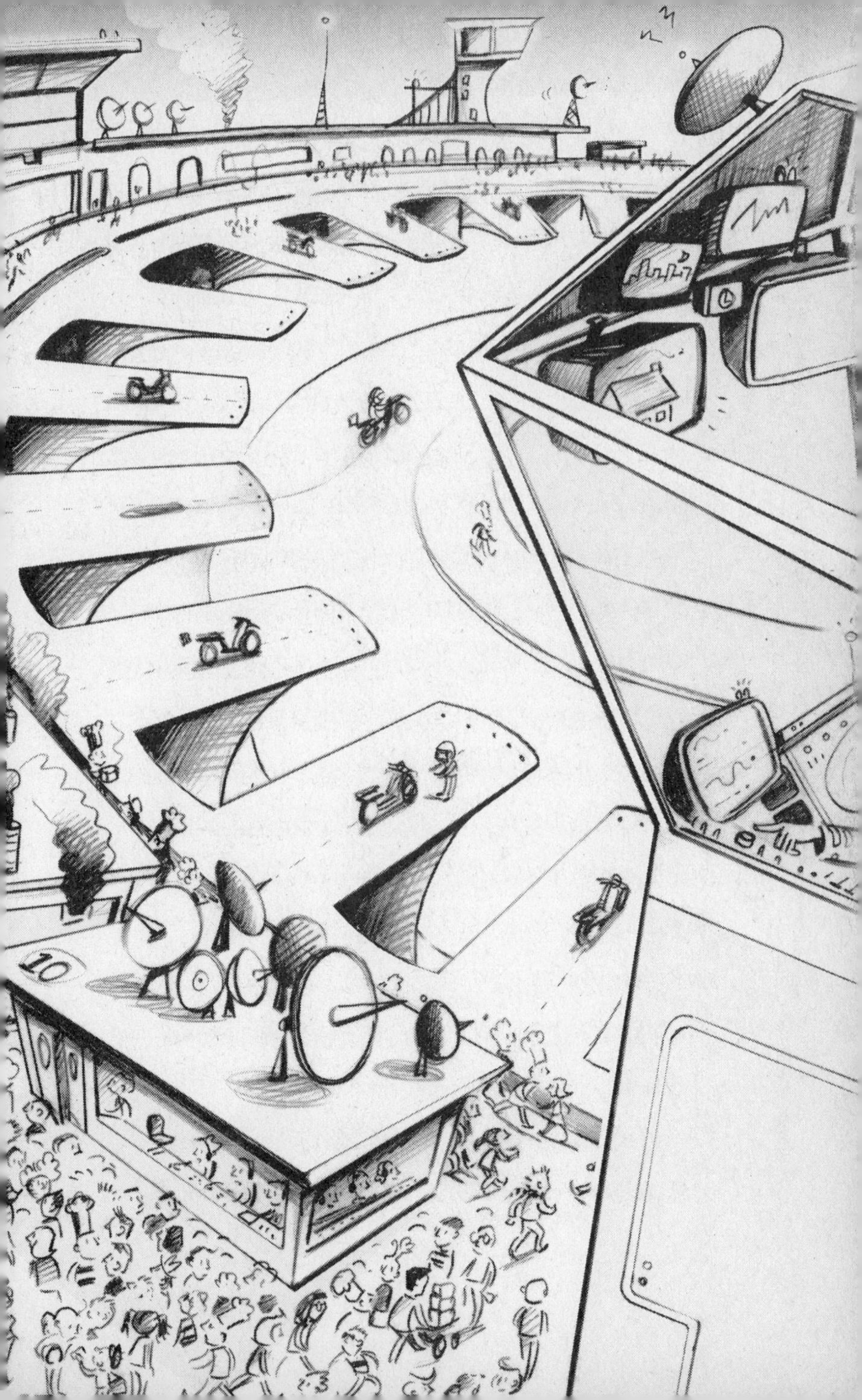
10

An awestruck young messenger was looking up at her. Quickly, Midge replaced her scowl with a smile. She knew how the messenger felt. Not so long ago, she had spent all her free time delivering messages around the Dream Centre, just to be close to the teams of Dream Fetchers she so admired.

"Thanks," she said, taking a folded slip of paper from the messenger's shaking hand. "Um. Good work."

The messenger beamed and darted away. Midge began to unfold the slip of paper.

"I think I see him!" yelled Harley. "Hey! Snaffle! Wait!"

Harley and Vert dashed off. Midge stuck the unopened message into her helmet and raced after them. As she dodged through the crowds, she was looking everywhere except straight ahead. When Motza, the Head Dream Chef, stepped out of the kitchens in a cloud of steam, she did not see him. Motza did not see Midge either. He was busy mopping his face with his apron.

"Watch out!" Harley cried, but she was too late. *Blam!* Midge and Motza collided. Midge flew backwards and landed on her back. She gazed up into

the roof space, trying to work out what had happened. All the breath was knocked out of her and the points of her ears were trembling with shock. Motza gave a surprised grunt and looked down to see who had run into him.

"Poor little Midge," he smiled, bending down to her. "That was quite a bump."

"Sorry, Mr Mozzarella, sir," Midge gasped.

"Not your fault," said Motza. "I, too, did not look where I was going. And please. You call me Motza. Everybody does." Gently, Motza set Midge back on her feet. "How do you feel?"

"Fine, thank you," said Midge. Motza peered at her closely. The points of her ears had stopped trembling and the colour had returned to her cheeks. Motza gave a satisfied nod and straightened up.

"In that case – go! Run! Vamoose!" he

said, frowning down at each of them in turn. "Hurry. She waits for you."

"Who?" asked Vert.

"Team Leader Flint," said Motza.

"But – that's who we're looking for," said Harley. "Her and Snaffle."

"You won't find your team leader here," said Motza.

"Why? Where is she?" Midge asked.

"At the launch pads, of course!" said Motza.

Midge turned to look at the other side of the Dream Centre, where the floor stopped and a huge, echoing chamber opened up. A long line of launch pads was fixed to the very edge of the floor so that they stuck out over the drop like the teeth of a huge comb. A stream of dreamskoots were taking off or coming in to land. They were all flying between the launch pads and a massive, circular frame set into the far wall of the Dream Centre. A shimmering film of shifting colours filled the frame like the liquid in a huge bubble wand. This was the gateway between Dreamside and Earthside.

"I see her!" Midge cried, spotting the familiar figure of Team Leader Flint on the metal walkway at the back of the launch pads. "But why is she waiting for us there? We're not flying for ages yet."

"Didn't you get her message?" Motza asked.

"Message...? Oh! Message!" As Midge reached into her helmet for the slip of paper, Vert gave a horrified groan.

"We're too late," he said, pointing a shaking finger at the launch pads. "Look."

Snaffle was on the metal walkway. He was striding towards Team Leader Flint with a determined look on his face.

"We'll never catch him now," Vert began, but he was talking to himself. Midge and Harley were already sprinting towards Snaffle. Vert set off after them.

It seemed to take for ever to fight their

way through the crowds. First they got stuck behind a squad of chefs carrying freshly baked dreams to the launch pads. Then they became tangled up with another group heading back to the kitchens. When they finally made it to the walkway, Snaffle had nearly reached Team Leader Flint.

"Snaffle! Remember your promise!" Harley yelled.

Snaffle ignored her and broke into a trot. They jumped onto the walkway and chased after him, their boots clanging on the metal. Team Leader Flint turned to see what all the noise was about. When she saw her trainees, she frowned.

"Even an urgent summons is no excuse for running on the walkway!" she snapped.

"Something to report, boss," Snaffle

panted, skidding to a halt.

"Don't you dare, *Snaffle*!" Midge shouted, catching up.

Harley bumped into Snaffle and Vert tottered into Midge. He grabbed her shoulder for support and pressed a hand to his side, trying to catch his breath.

"What *is* going on here?" said Team Leader Flint in a voice sharp enough to slice through steel.

They all began talking at once.

"It's about Vert—"

"Shut up, Snaffle!"

"He's just angry because of the letter—"

"Please. I can manage. My parents..."

"SILENCE!"

Team Leader Flint's bellow was loud enough to send echoes bouncing around the chamber. They all snapped to attention.

"Whatever this is," said Team Leader Flint, glaring at each of them in turn, "we don't have time to sort it out now."

"But—" Snaffle began.

"I said it will have to wait!"

"But Vert is scared of—"

"The next one to speak will have fifty points deducted from their score."

Midge held her breath. Team Leader Flint raised her eyebrows at Snaffle, who opened his mouth, then pressed his lips together and scowled. Midge breathed a sigh of relief. Vert was safe. For now.

Team Leader Flint brought her clipboard out from under her arm. "Listen up, Dream Team. I sent for you early because the Earthside weather forecast is not good. The skies are clear now but there are blizzards moving in. I want you back here in Dreamside before the first Earthside snowflake falls. So I have rescheduled your speed challenge. You take off in three minutes."

"Th-three..?" Vert began to tremble. Midge shuffled sideways until he was hidden behind her, but Team Leader Flint was too busy handing out fur-lined overcoats to notice Vert's shivers.

"Put these on," she ordered. "It's below freezing Earthside. I have already selected four dream orders for you. You're going at a time when most adult humans are still awake, so your customers on this mission are all children. Each delivery address is exactly – and I mean exactly – the same distance from the gateway, so you all have an equal chance of winning the speed challenge. Aha! Here they come."

Four chefs were marching towards them, each carrying a flat cardboard box. Midge grinned with excitement as

she pulled on her overcoat. Soon she would be delivering one of those dreams.

"Now remember," Team Leader Flint continued. "The speed challenge is only about how fast you can fly. Once you reach your delivery address, we stop the clock until you start flying again. So please, do not take any risks with your deliveries. Take your time. Do your safety checks. Plan your escape routes. And what do we always say?"

"Makes you shiver? Don't deliver," they chorused obediently.

"Good. And if anyone is still Earthside when it starts to snow, you must use your N.A.P. Understood?"

Midge grimaced. Beside her, Harley gave a scornful snort. Snaffle folded his arms rebelliously. Even Vert looked doubtful. Every dreamskoot was fitted with a N.A.P., which stood for Neutral Atmosphere Provider. Any Dream Fetcher caught Earthside in bad weather could activate their N.A.P. and seal themselves inside a protective bubble. The N.A.P. forcefield was so strong that Earthside wind, rain or snow simply passed right around it. But a N.A.P. used up a lot of dreamskoot power. Any Dream Fetcher using it could only glide very slowly home, which was no good at all in a speed challenge.

"I mean it!" Team Leader Flint warned, seeing their reluctant faces. "Don't even think about taking any risks out there. Some of those Earthside snowflakes are bigger than your silly, fat heads. One more thing." She pointed to the roof space above the launch pads. The Three Abiding Rules were written there in gold letters.

Midge looked up and felt a guilty flush spread right to the points of her ears. The Three Abiding Rules were what every Dream Fetcher lived by. Anyone caught breaking an Abiding Rule on purpose was instantly dismissed. On her first solo flight, Midge had managed to break all three. During her navigation test she had deliberately broken Rule One again. Even worse, she had persuaded Vert to help her. Luckily for her, Team Leader Flint had not found out. Now, as she gazed at the glittering words above her head, Midge promised herself that she would complete her speed challenge without breaking any of the Abiding Rules.

"Well?" Team Leader Flint snapped, making them jump. "What are you waiting for? To your dreamskoots!"

Midge hurried to her launch pad and jumped into the saddle. The chef had already slotted her dream delivery into the padded holder on the back of her dreamskoot. Midge pressed her thumb against the identity pad on the dashboard control panel. She felt a tingle as her thumbprint was scanned and then one of the screens on the control panel lit up.

> Welcome, Midge. Ready to go?

Midge turned to the rest of her dream

team. "Good luck!" she called across the launch pads.

Vert gave her a terrified smile. Snaffle sent her a furious glare. Harley raised both hands in an excited thumbs-up. Midge eased her helmet down over her ears and switched on her dreamcom.

"Begin launch procedure," Team Leader Flint ordered into the earpiece.

"Yes, boss," said Midge. "Power up."

Her dreamskoot began to hum with energy.

"Lift off."

Her dreamskoot rose into the air and hovered above the launch pad.

"Wings out."

A pair of paper-thin, silvery wings opened out from beneath the footplates.

"Earthside!" said Midge.

Her dreamskoot surged forward and she headed straight for the gateway in the far wall, with Vert, Harley and Snaffle right beside her.

Squelch! They all hit the gateway together. Midge squeezed her eyes shut and held her breath as she passed through to Earthside. It was a very strange feeling. She had never been pulled through a vat of warm jelly, but she thought that passing through the gateway must be a pretty close match.

Glop! One by one they flew out the other side of the gateway, which was hidden in a pile of stones on a hilltop. It was a freezing cold night Earthside. Snow lay thick on the ground but the sky was clear and full of stars. Below them, the rooftops of an Earthside town glittered frostily in the moonlight. A silvery river ran through the middle of the town, passing under three graceful bridges before it reached the sea.

For a few seconds, Midge forgot all about the speed challenge.

"Isn't it beautiful?" she sighed, gazing down at the snow-covered town. There was no answer. Snaffle and Harley had both zoomed off towards their delivery addresses without a backward glance. Even Vert wasn't hanging around. He had dropped as low to the ground as he could and was making his slightly wobbly way inland. Midge looked at her control panel. Her speed challenge timer had already started. The green-lit seconds were ticking away.

"Concentrate, Midge!" she snapped, frowning at her map screen. There were three coloured dots on it. The blue dot was the gateway behind her, the green dot was her dreamskoot and the red dot marked the location of her customer. Midge put her head down and opened up the throttle.

She flew as fast and straight as an

arrow and did not slow down until she reached the red dot on her map screen. As she brought her dreamskoot to a halt, Midge glanced at her speed challenge timer and smiled proudly. If she could do as well on the return flight, she might just manage to beat Harley for once. But first, she had a dream to deliver.

Midge looked down. She was hovering above a wood. She searched the snowy treetops, expecting to find a clearing with a house standing in the middle of it. There was no clearing. Midge turned her dreamskoot in a circle, looking for a chimney stack or the orange glow of a lighted window. She saw nothing but trees. Midge frowned. According to the map screen she was directly above her customer, but where was the house?

Maybe it isn't a house, thought Midge, remembering the circus caravan she and Harley had visited on their navigation test. Perhaps this customer lived in a caravan too. Midge put her dreamskoot into a dive. It was time to take a look below the treetops.

It was much darker in the wood. Midge flicked on her headlight. The tiny beam of light showed tree trunks crowding in from all sides. Midge gave a puzzled sigh. There was no room in this wood for even the smallest caravan. She checked her customer details. The dream had been ordered by an eight-year-old boy called Cameron. His address was –

Midge stared at the screen. There was no address. Instead there were just two words: `> In transit.` Midge began to feel worried. "In transit" dream orders were not unusual. Humans tended to fall asleep all over the place. But Cameron was only eight years old. What was he doing out in the woods without any shelter on a night when the temperature was below freezing?

Something moaned near by. Midge shot back up into the trees. She peered down from the shelter of a snow-covered branch. There was nothing to be seen. Except… Midge tilted her head to one side. Something had made deep parallel gouges in one patch of ground. Midge edged closer and saw that the ground dropped away suddenly into a narrow ravine. Whatever had made the gouges had tried to cling to the edge of the drop – and failed. She could see a trail of snapped branches and dislodged rocks all the way down into the blackness at the bottom of the ravine.

Midge hesitated. *"Makes you shiver? Don't deliver,"* she whispered, staring down into the darkness. Another moan sounded from below, much weaker than the first. Just for an instant, Midge wished she could be more like Snaffle. Snaffle did not care one bit about humans. He would turn around now and head back to Dreamside without a backward glance. But Midge could not do it. She blew a wisp of hair out of her eyes and eased her dreamskoot down into the ravine.

There was a frozen stream at the bottom. A dark shape was lying next to the stream – a human boy! Midge edged closer and shone her headlight beam onto his face. His eyes were closed, his skin was pale and his lips were blue with cold. There was a big bruise on his forehead. Bringing her dreamskoot as close as she dared, Midge leant out of the saddle and pressed her hand against his cheek. He was as cold as marble. If he stayed there much longer he would freeze to death.

Midge flew across to his ear. "Cameron!" she shouted. "Wake up!"

Cameron did not move. Midge grabbed a handful of his hair and yanked on it as hard as she could. His eyelids did not even flutter.

Midge thought hard. How could she wake him? Her eyes brightened as an idea came to her. If Cameron had ordered a nightmare, it might just be scary enough to do the trick. She yanked the dream box from the padded holder on the back of her dreamskoot and read the label.

"Puppies and chocolate."

Midge sighed. Puppies and chocolate did not sound like nightmare ingredients to her. She dropped the dream box onto Cameron's chest and watched it disappear with a tiny *Phut!* The dream began to play and Cameron smiled in his deep, cold sleep. Midge nearly cried as she hovered over him. She had never felt so helpless.

A stone clattered behind her. Midge spun her dreamskoot round but there was nothing to see except a pile of earth and rocks. Cameron must have caused a small landslide when he fell. As Midge stared, another pebble wobbled and moved at the edge of the pile. A third stone was pushed away, then a fourth. Something was coming out of the ground.

Midge was terrified. She wanted to fly away, but she could not leave Cameron all alone. Instead, she turned her dreamskoot until its headlight beam lit up the patch of moving earth. Then Midge did something very brave. She switched off her headlight and waited in the darkness, listening to the rattle of pebbles and the whisper of shifting soil. When the Earthside creature appeared, she planned to frighten it away by switching on her headlight and shining the beam right into its eyes. If her plan didn't work – well, Midge did not even want to think about that.

There was just enough moonlight for Midge to see something climbing out of the hole it had made. She got ready to switch on her headlight but then stopped short with her finger frozen above the button. It was not an Earthside creature climbing from the hole. It was a Collector. Midge let out a shaky breath and sat back in her saddle, weak with relief.

Collectors came from Dreamside, just like her. They lived deep underground in The Below. Their job was to collect raw dream ingredients from Earthside and take them back to the Dream Kitchens. Collectors had their own gateways leading from Dreamside through to a sprawling network of Earthside tunnels. The tunnels were just big enough for the collector's carts to trundle along as they moved between collecting caverns. Each cavern had been hollowed out under an Earthside place that was full of strong human feelings. The feelings seeped down through the earth and into filter pipes drilled into the cavern roof. Finally, the distilled human feelings dripped from the end of the pipes and into the waiting carts below.

Midge knew that Collectors were a vital part of dream-making but she found it hard to like them. Long ago, Collectors had moved freely between the surface of Dreamside and The Below, but slowly they had grown to prefer the dark. Now Collectors and their families rarely came to the surface. Their pale eyes and mushroom-white skin could not tolerate daylight. Midge knew that other Dream Fetchers had Collector friends and were quite happy to take the long elevator ride down to The Below to visit them, but she preferred to stay above ground.

"Hello, Midge," said a sweet, high voice.

Midge jumped. "How do you know my name?" she demanded, frowning at the young Collector, who had now climbed from the hole and was sitting on the edge, swinging her legs.

"It's written on your uniform badge," said the Collector.

Midge tried to read the Collector's name badge, but she could not make it out in the gloom of the ravine. "It might seem as bright as day to you," she said, a little resentfully. "But I can't quite see to read your name."

"Velvet," said the young Collector. "My name is Velvet. Because of this," she added, running a hand over the top of her head. Her thick, blue-black hair was cut in the Collector way, cropped short on top with one long plait running down her back. "Feel it," said Velvet, bending the top of her head towards Midge.

Midge hesitated. The thought of touching a Collector made her shudder.

"Go on!"

Midge leant down from the saddle of her dreamskoot and ran her hand over Velvet's cropped hair. It was warm and – well, velvety.

"See?" laughed Velvet. "My dad says it's like a mole's back. And he should know. He met a mole once – and lived to tell the tale."

"Why are you here?" asked Midge.

"Tunnel cave-in," said Velvet, pointing down the hole. "This topside earthslide must've done it. I shouldn't be above ground, though," she whispered, leaning closer to Midge. "Too curious about Earthside, see. I'm always getting into trouble."

"Me too!" said Midge, surprised to find that she had something in common with a Collector.

"I'll have to close this tunnel down, I reckon," said Velvet. "It's too near the surface now. That stream has worn away a lot of rock over the centuries."

As Velvet chatted on, Midge studied her in the faint moonlight. Really she was not too bad to look at. Her eyes were a pretty silvery colour and her white skin went well with her black hair. Her ears were rather large but at least they were nicely pointed.

"What about you?" Velvet finished. "Why are you here?"

"I'm delivering a dream to this human boy, but he's—"

"There's a human here?" Velvet gasped.

"Just behind me," said Midge. "He's called Cameron. Didn't you see him?"

"Collectors can see well in the dark, but we can't see very far," said Velvet. "We don't often need to. Down in the tunnels we use hearing rather than sight," she added, pointing to her large ears. "Is it safe to be this close? He might wake up."

"He's more than asleep. He's unconscious," said Midge. "And he's very cold. If he stays here much longer, he might die. I don't know what to do," she finished miserably.

Velvet walked up to Cameron and touched his cold hand. "Hmm. I suppose I could try Tempo-seal."

"Tempo-what?"

Velvet pulled something from her belt and held it up for Midge to see. It was a silver rod with a handle at one end. Velvet pressed a button on the handle.

The rod began to hum with energy and a faint blue glow appeared. "It's a Weaver. We use them to weave a temporary energy seal across a tunnel breach. If I could weave a Tempo-seal cocoon around Cameron, it would keep him warm at least."

"Could you weave enough energy to cover something as big as a human?" Midge asked.

"I think so," said Velvet, standing back and staring up at Cameron's side. "If only I could reach high enough."

"What if I gave you a lift?" Midge asked, patting the back of her saddle.

Velvet's silvery eyes sparkled with excitement. "I've always wanted to ride a dreamskoot!" she laughed, reaching up to grasp Midge's outstretched hand. Midge was surprised to discover that Velvet's hand was not cold and slimy, but warm and dry just like hers. She tightened her grip and pulled Velvet up to sit behind her.

Midge flew down to Cameron's feet and then zigzagged all the way up his body. Behind her, Velvet wove a net of glowing blue strands. When Midge reached Cameron's head, Velvet tied off the last strand and the completed net floated down to cover him like a blanket.

"You did it!" said Midge. "Look! His lips are pinking up already–"

"Shhh!"

Midge turned in the saddle. Velvet was listening. Her large ears quivered as she picked up a distant sound.

"Dog," said Velvet. "There's a dog barking in the woods. I don't like dogs. They dig," she said, darkly.

"I can't hear it," said Midge.

"It's coming closer. There are humans with it. They're calling Cameron's name."

"A search party?" Midge cried. "Cameron's going to be found!"

Velvet shook her head. "I don't think so. They think the dog is taking them to Cameron but the stupid thing is just chasing around having fun."

"I thought you said they were getting closer?" said Midge.

"They were, but they're going away

again now. The silly dog is taking them that way," said Velvet, pointing in one direction. "No, hang on," she added, tilting her head in the opposite direction. "Now it's going that way."

Midge looked down at Cameron. "Then we'd better bring the dog here," she said.

"How are we going to do that?" Velvet asked.

"We'll give it something to chase!" Midge yelled, opening up the throttle of her dreamskoot.

They raced through the moonlit wood towards the barking dog, dodging tree trunks and soaring over bushes. Velvet was whooping with delight at the roller-coaster ride but Midge was frowning as she steered her dreamskoot through the trees at top speed. She was thinking about the time ticking away on her speed challenge clock now that she had left the ravine. More importantly, she was worrying about how to bring the humans to Cameron without breaking the third Abiding Rule. *Never be seen.*

A dog doesn't count, she told herself. *If I let the dog see me but stay hidden from the humans, I won't be breaking any rules.*

Midge dodged another tree trunk, still worrying, and nearly ran headfirst into the dog. It was big, with sharp white fangs and thick curved claws. Midge turned steeply and shot around the back of the tree again while the dog was still snuffling under a bush.

"Here," she whispered to Velvet, yanking off her helmet. "Put this on. The visor is tinted. It'll protect your eyes from the light."

"What light?" Velvet asked.

"I'm going to use my headlight to attract the dog. Ready?"

For answer, Velvet pulled on the helmet and wrapped her arms firmly around Midge's waist.

"Here goes," Midge muttered.

She flew out from behind the tree and flashed her headlight at the dog. It looked up and then leapt straight for her with its jaws open wide. *Snap!* Its fangs closed on empty air. Midge was

already hovering beside the next tree. She set off back to the ravine, dodging from tree to tree. The dog ran after her, barking all the way. The humans stumbled and floundered after the dog, never quite catching up enough to see the little dreamskoot whizzing through the trees.

When she was nearly there, Midge put on an extra spurt of speed. She shot down into the ravine ahead of the dog

and landed her dreamskoot beside the hole that led down to Velvet's tunnel.

"That was fun!" Velvet laughed as she jumped down from the dreamskoot and handed the helmet back to Midge.

"You call that fun?" said Midge. "You remind me of my friend Harley."

"It was great. In fact, you know the only bad thing about tonight?"

"What?"

"That stupid dog is going to be a hero. It'll be in all the Earthside papers tomorrow. 'Boy saved by faithful pet.' Nobody will ever know what we did. Oh – that reminds me." Velvet pulled her Weaver from her belt. "I'd better get rid of the Tempo-seal."

The dog was getting nearer and the humans weren't far behind. Midge could see torchlight through the trees. She hovered anxiously as Velvet pointed the

Weaver at Cameron's blanket and pressed a button on the handle. *Pffft!* The glowing blue strands shrivelled up and disappeared. Suddenly uncovered, Cameron frowned and curled up into a ball. "Don't want to go to school," he muttered.

"He's coming round," said Midge, with a relieved smile.

"And he sounds just like my little brother," said Velvet. "Fancy us having something in common. Who would've thought it?"

"That's just how I feel," said Midge, laughing down at

the little Collector. “Who would've thought it?”

Velvet slid down into the hole. “You know the best thing about tonight?” she called up to Midge. “I made a new friend.”

“Me too,” said Midge.

“Bye for now!” Velvet sealed the tunnel behind her just as the dog tumbled down into the ravine with slaver flying from its jaws.

“Bye, Velvet!” called Midge, heading for the treetops. “See you again!” And she meant it.

Fish Food

Snaffle was so full of rage, he thought he might burst. As he raced towards his delivery address, he imagined two jets of rage blasting from his shoulder blades and spreading a white-hot trail across the sky. He imagined the humans in the town below looking up at him and thinking they were seeing a shooting star.

Stupid humans, wishing on a star that wasn't there! What was the point of wishing anyway? Wishes never came true. He had wished for a Good Luck card, and what had he got? Snaffle scowled. He had to win more points somehow. He turned in his saddle and glared back at the Earthside hilltop, wishing he could send a jet of rage right through the gateway and into the Dream Centre to knock Team Leader Flint off her stupid feet. When he got back to Dreamside he would make her listen to his news about Vert!

As for his dream team, they were so stupid they ought to win a prize. Fancy thinking points didn't matter! Fancy thinking they could all be one happy family! Snaffle was ashamed to admit that he had begun to believe them. Luckily his father's letter had arrived just in time to put a stop to all that nonsense.

Snaffle tried to check his position on his map screen but his eyes were watering too much to see properly. Stupid icy wind! He reached up to slam his visor into place but his hand bumped against glass. His visor was already down. Furiously, he blinked the tears away. His speed challenge timer swam into focus. Snaffle smiled. He was making excellent time. A second later his smile faded. Excellent wasn't good enough. He had to be the best.

He pressed a button to change the on-screen view. Now the map showed four helmet icons, one for each member of his dream team. The helmets marked "M"

and "V" were way behind, but the helmet marked with an "H" showed that Harley was zooming towards her delivery address as fast as he was. Snaffle needed more speed.

He bent forward until his chest was pressed against the saddle. It was an uncomfortable way to fly but it made him more streamlined. He turned his handlebar throttle as far as it would go and held it there. His dreamskoot surged forward, faster and faster, until the whole machine began to shake. The rush of wind across his wings became a shrill scream. Snaffle gritted his teeth and hung on.

By the time he reached his delivery address, the engine of his dreamskoot had begun to whine in protest. He slowed to a stop and hovered outside his customer's house. The little machine creaked and shuddered as it cooled down. The wings fluttered in a tired way. Snaffle felt a twinge of guilt but quickly squashed it. The Dreamside mechanics would fix any damage to his dreamskoot. That was their job. His job was to win the speed challenge. He checked Harley's position on the screen. She was just arriving at her delivery address. He had beaten her by seconds! If he could match his speed on the flight back to Dreamside, he would win the speed challenge. But first he had to make his delivery.

His customer lived in a bungalow. Deliveries to bungalows were always risky. All the rooms were on one level, which meant there was more danger of bumping into a human or, even worse, a pet. At one end of the house, light streamed out from a pair of patio doors. Snaffle checked it out. Two adult humans were sitting

together on the sofa watching television. There were no pets in sight.

Snaffle gave a satisfied nod. The humans looked settled for the evening. He cruised along to the bedrooms at the other end of the bungalow. The curtains were closed at his customer's window but there was a gap big enough to peer through. In the room beyond, the light from a large fish tank shone across a bed where a dark-haired boy lay sleeping. Snaffle double-checked his order details and nodded. The customer was a ten-year-old boy called Samir.

Snaffle was about to close down the order page when something caught his eye. He stopped and frowned at the screen. Samir had ordered a nightmare. Snaffle did not care about that – dream or nightmare, it was all the same to him. But this particular nightmare delivery came with a complication. There was a red "Screamer" alert flashing at the bottom of the screen.

"Great," muttered Snaffle, glaring in at the sleeping boy. "A Screamer. Just what I need."

Nightmare deliveries were plagued by two main types of Screamers. The first type screamed themselves awake. The second type stayed asleep but screamed so loudly, they woke up other humans. Either way, they were trouble. A Dream Fetcher delivering a nightmare to a Screamer ran a much higher risk of being seen. Snaffle sighed and began looking for a way in. More importantly, he began looking for a quick way out again.

Samir's bedroom window was shut but the bathroom window next door was open just wide enough for a dreamskoot to squeeze through. Snaffle checked that Samir's bedroom door was open and then he eased through the bathroom window. He hovered there with his head poking above the sill. The bathroom was dark and empty. The door to the hallway was open.

Snaffle thought about it. Samir could start to scream at any time once the nightmare was delivered. Would he have time to fly out of the bedroom, shoot along the hallway, zip into the bathroom and escape through the open window before Samir's parents came running from the other end of the bungalow? He edged outside again and looked along the length of the building, judging how far the humans would have to run. Snaffle nodded. Yes, he could do it.

This time he eased right through the gap and into the bathroom. The air was warm and damp and smelled of pine needles. A tap was dripping into the basin below the window with a hollow *plink-plink-plink*. Snaffle flew across to the doorway. He edged around the door frame. A lamp glowed halfway down the long hallway, revealing other bedroom doors. They were all shut. He checked the carpeted floor. No cats or dogs and no sign of pet hairs or chewed-up toys.

"Here goes," muttered Snaffle. He took a deep breath and shot around the corner into Samir's bedroom.

Once inside, he flew up to the safety of the ceiling and hovered there while he looked around. The fish tank in the middle of the room was nearly as long as Samir's bed. The green-lit water was swarming with fish. There were darting silver shoals with bright neon flashes along their sides and some jolly, round fish striped with vertical bands of black, orange and white. Two glittering beauties paraded like movie stars,

trailing long, lacy fins behind them. On the bottom of the tank, a fat catfish trundled about, looking for food in the gravel. Two feelers hung from its mouth like an over-long moustache.

Snaffle did not spend long checking out the fish. Unlike most human pets, they were not a threat to him. The only problem with the tank was the bright glow it was sending out. The light made it difficult for him to see into the gloomy corners of the room. He tried listening instead. He could hear the watery burble of the fish-tank pump and Samir's steady breathing from the bed by the window. He was about to fly down to make his delivery when he heard a third sound. Over in the corner behind the door, someone snored.

Very slowly, Snaffle turned towards the sound. There was a second bed in the room. He had not seen it from the window because it had been hidden by the fish tank. An older boy was lying on the bed, snoring gently. Samir shared a bedroom with his brother.

Snaffle hesitated. Common sense told him to abandon this delivery. He was only a trainee. Nobody would expect him to deliver a nightmare to a Screamer when there was another human in the room.

Nobody but his father. He would expect nothing less than perfection. Snaffle knew just how their next meeting would go if he didn't make this delivery.

"So, Snaffle," his father would say. "I hear you finally won something?"

"Yes, father. I had the fastest time in the speed challenge."

"Didn't quite manage to deliver that nightmare though, did you, son?"

"No, but it was a Screamer—"

"Never mind. We can't all be as good as your brother Grabble, can we?"

Snaffle scowled. How many times had he heard his father say that? Well, here was his chance to prove that he was as good as Grabble. Before he could lose his nerve, he zoomed down and flicked the nightmare box onto Samir's chest.

Phut! The nightmare sank in and disappeared. Snaffle turned his dreamskoot and set off towards the door. He needed to be back outside before –

"GAAHHH!"

Snaffle nearly fell out of his saddle. He looked over his shoulder. Samir was

sitting bolt upright in bed. Snaffle could not believe how quickly the screaming had started. Should he fly or hide? He decided to keep flying.

"AAARRRGGGHHH!!!" Samir screamed again. "NNNOOOO!"

Snaffle cleared the top of the fish tank and then stopped so suddenly, he nearly flipped over his handlebars. Samir's brother was awake. He was climbing out of bed. His feet were already on the floor. When he stood up, they would be nose to nose. Snaffle didn't stop to think. He dived – and plunged straight into the fish tank.

As soon as his dreamskoot hit the water it switched to aqua-mode. The exhaust pipes sealed shut, the back wheel swivelled round to act as a propeller and the wings began to move gently up and down like fins. Snaffle was not so quick to react. Team Leader Flint had drilled them in survival procedures for every possible emergency. He had spent a few very wet hours in the Dream Centre pool, learning exactly what to do if he fell into water. Unfortunately, the shock of finding himself inside the fish tank had driven all thoughts from his head. He simply sat there, clinging to his handlebars as his dreamskoot settled into the gravel at the bottom of the tank.

After a few seconds of frozen panic, Snaffle calmed down enough to realize that he was not drowning. From the neck down he was as wet as a herring, but his head was poking up into a pocket of air inside his helmet. Snaffle took grateful little sips of the air. He had enough oxygen to keep him alive while he figured out what to do next. Meanwhile, he would have to keep very still to make sure the air pocket stayed inside his helmet –

Blam! Something knocked against the front wheel of his dreamskoot. He tilted sideways and a bubble of air escaped from his helmet before he could straighten up again. Now the water was up to his chin. Very carefully, Snaffle turned his head to see what had hit him. He came face to face with the catfish. Its huge head was three times as big as his, including his helmet. It had bulging eyes, warty skin and a wide, blubbery mouth. It looked like a cross between a frog and his grandfather.

Snaffle tried to scream, but as soon as he opened his mouth, water poured in. It tasted horrible. He spluttered and swallowed and then gave a disgusted groan. Most of the fish in the tank were swimming around with long threads of poo hanging from their bottoms. It stood to reason. He must have swallowed some fish poo along with the water. And what about fish wee? *Did* fish wee?

The catfish rose up to the level of his helmet and stared in at him with bulging eyes.

"Get lost, fish face!" cried Snaffle through clenched teeth as he struggled to keep his chin above water.

The catfish dipped its whiskery snout and gave the front wheel a second hard nudge. Again the dreamskoot tilted and another bubble of air escaped from Snaffle's helmet. He rammed his heel into the gravel and pushed himself upright. This time, the water level was just under his nose. In desperation, he rammed his foot out sideways and landed a lucky kick. The startled catfish shot off to hide inside a nearby plant.

Snaffle sagged with relief and then quickly sat up again as his nostrils filled with water. *Come on!* he thought. *What's the emergency procedure after falling into water?* His mind remained stubbornly blank. Above him, a brightly striped fish was closing in. One of the movie star fish drifted into view, trailing its glittering shawls and eyeing him hungrily. The catfish came out of hiding and, once again, headed for his front wheel. Snaffle groaned. One more nudge from the catfish and the last bubble of air would escape from his helmet. Unless the striped fish bit his head off first. This was no time for his brain to take a nap. Nap...?

"N.A.P.!" yelled Snaffle, blowing a stream of bubbles. He slammed his palm down onto a red button on his control panel. Instantly, his dreamskoot's Neutral Atmosphere Provider sprang into action. The force field pushed the water back and, all of

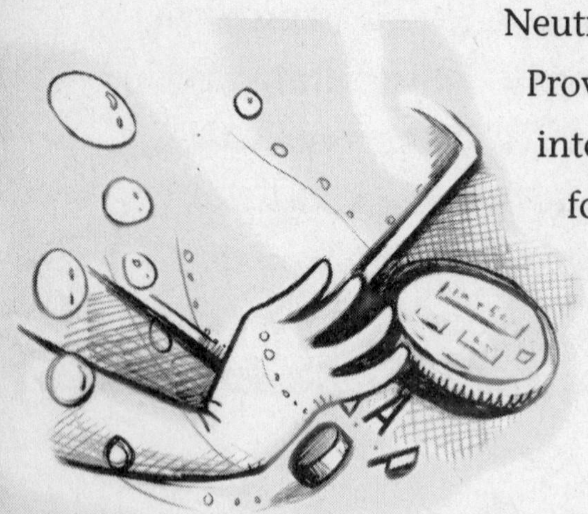

a sudden, he was sitting on his dreamskoot inside a protective bubble of air. Water drained from his helmet and poured out of his soaking clothes to form a pond on the floor of the bubble.

"Hah!" yelled Snaffle, as all the fish turned tail and darted away from the shockwave. "You stupid scaredy-pants! That'll teach you to mess with a Dream Fetcher!" A crazed laugh escaped him as he pointed his dreamskoot upwards. He had nearly been fish food. The relief made him feel light-headed.

He brought his dreamskoot to a stop just under the surface. His next challenge was to find somewhere safe and warm to dry out his clothes. He could not win the speed challenge if he kept his N.A.P. on all the way home, but if he tried to fly through the cold Earthside night dripping wet and without the protection of the force field, he would probably freeze solid. He could hide out in the bathroom airing cupboard and dry his clothes on the hot-water tank. But first he had to get out of the bedroom unseen.

He peered through the glass wall of the fish tank, trying to see what Samir and his brother were up to. Samir was sitting on his bed, crying. There was no sign of the older brother.

"He's walked out on you, hasn't he," whispered Snaffle, remembering how Grabble used to march out and leave him alone in the dark when he woke up crying from a bad dream. "But he's doing it for your own good, you know. Nobody likes a coward. You have to toughen up." He watched Samir's miserable face through the glass for a while and then shook himself into action. He edged his dreamskoot through the water until the open feeding hatch was right above him. It was slow progress with the N.A.P. taking up most of the power, but once his dreamskoot was out of the water he would be able to turn off the force field. "Here goes," he muttered, opening the throttle.

Boing! Snaffle hit the glass wall of the tank. He tried again. This time he bobbed up to the surface and then rose slowly out of the water. As soon as he was clear he closed down his N.A.P. The dreamskoot switched to full power, picked up speed and shot out through the hatch. He flew across the bedroom, dripping all the way.

At the door, Snaffle edged his dreamskoot forward and checked the hallway. He was looking forward to recovering in the warm darkness of the airing cupboard, but he was in for a shock. Samir's big brother had gone to get the other humans. All three of them were striding along the hallway. In a moment they would reach the bedroom.

Snaffle reversed and gazed around the room in a panic. He had to find somewhere to hide! But where? If he could get behind the curtains he might be safe, but Samir was still crouched on the edge of his bed, directly in front of the gap. Snaffle took a risk. He zoomed over Samir's bowed head and shot through the gap in the curtains. An instant later, the bedroom light was switched on. He landed his dreamskoot on the windowsill and took a few calming deep breaths. That had been far too close for his liking.

There was a radiator directly below the windowsill. Snaffle took off his fur-lined overcoat and hung it from the back of his saddle. The heated air began to dry his uniform and he settled back to watch the human family through the gap in the curtains.

The brother was leaning against the fish tank gazing sleepily at the fish. *Good job I didn't stay in there,* Snaffle thought. He turned his attention to the mother and father. They were standing by the bed looking down at Samir. *Now he's for it,* Snaffle thought. *His father will tell him nobody likes a coward, the mother will refuse to give him a cuddle and his brother will demand to sleep in another room.*

"Come here," said the mother, sitting down on the bed.

Samir pushed his face into his mother's shoulder and she wrapped him in her arms. Behind the curtain, Snaffle shook his head in amazement.

"What do you call a three-legged donkey?" said the father, handing Samir a tissue.

"Da-ad!" said Samir, wiping the tears from his face.

"Wonky," said the father. "Do you get it? Three-legged donkey? Wonky?"

"Shut up, Dad," said Samir, rewarding his father with just a hint of a smile.

"What do you call a one-eyed, three-legged donkey?" asked the father.

"Da-ad!" said Samir.

"Winky Wonky," said the father.

Samir laughed. Snaffle frowned. Was this human father crazy?

Samir looked over at his brother. "Sorry for waking you up," he whispered.

Here it comes, thought Snaffle, waiting for the brother to demand another bed for the night.

"Don't be daft," said the brother. "I wasn't even asleep."

Snaffle's mouth formed a perfect "O" of surprise. Now the brother was lying to make Samir feel better! What was wrong with this family? They reminded him of his dream team. All lovey-dovey and pretending to care. He tried to sneer but his top lip was a bit too wobbly to manage it. He felt a tightening in his chest.

"You know the best cure for a nightmare?" said Samir's mum. "Ice cream! Come on. Let's go get some."

The whole family left the bedroom and headed for the kitchen, arm in arm. As Snaffle watched them go, he felt his chest tighten even more. He shuffled uncomfortably. His chest was not the only part of him that was suffering. His neck felt as though invisible hands were gripping it, his shoulders were in a vice and his bottom was definitely feeling the pinch. He looked down at himself and gave a horrified groan.

"My uniform!"

His beautifully tailored uniform had shrunk so much, it now looked as though it had been sprayed on. The trouser bottoms were up to his shins and the sleeve cuffs were trying to squeeze past his elbows. The specially added shoulder pads had shrivelled up so much it looked as though he had a pair of potatoes sitting on his shoulders. He looked down just in time to see his jacket part company with his trousers, leaving his belly sticking out for the whole world to see. He yanked at the waistband but that only made matters worse. With a horrible ripping sound, his trousers split up the backside.

Snaffle was furious. His uniform was not a cheap, off-the-peg affair. It had been made especially for him at great expense. This whole mess was the stupid tailor's fault. How dare he use shoddy material that shrank at the slightest hint of damp! Just then, Snaffle had an uncomfortable flashback. He remembered how the tailor had hovered anxiously at his elbow as he pointed out a roll of exquisite cloth.

"But young sir, that is dry-clean only," the tailor had said.

"I don't care," he had replied. "That's the material I want for my uniform."

Snaffle pushed the memory aside. It was still the tailor's fault. The stupid man should have talked him out of it. When he returned to Dreamside he was going to go straight to that tailor and –

A look of horror spread across Snaffle's face. How could he return to Dreamside looking like he had squeezed himself into a baby's sleepsuit? He gazed desperately around as though he might find a spare Dream Fetcher uniform laid out on the windowsill. He spotted something nearly as good. His fur-lined overcoat was still hanging from the back of his saddle.

Gratefully, Snaffle grabbed the coat and pulled it on. He groaned. The coat had shrunk but the fur lining had not. Now he looked like an overstuffed teddy bear, with tufts of fur bulging out everywhere. He gave a resigned shrug. At least his bare bottom was covered up.

Laughter sounded from the other end of the hallway. It was time to get out of the bungalow before the humans came back. He made his way to the bathroom and flew across to the open window. He hovered there for a moment, looking out at the snowy scene beyond. The sky was still clear above the bungalow, but there was a bank of thick cloud building up in the west. The snow was moving in but Snaffle did not have time to worry about that. He had something more important to think about. As soon as he slipped through the window, he would be outside the bungalow and his speed challenge clock would start ticking again.

Snaffle frowned with determination. He might look like a clown but he was deadly serious about doing his best on this mission. He had already completed a risky delivery without breaking any of the Abiding Rules. Now it was time to win the speed challenge. He slammed down his helmet visor, took a firm grip on his handlebars and opened up the throttle.

"Eat my dust, Harley!" he yelled as he zipped across the night sky, heading back to Dreamside as fast as he could fly.

The Raggedy Doll

Harley was fizzing with excitement as she sped towards her delivery address. She had been up for hours before breakfast, racing her dreamskoot around the Dreamside sky-track and fine-tuning its engine. Now, finally, the speed challenge was under way. Harley grinned as she skimmed over the snow-covered rooftops. This was why she was training to be a Dream Fetcher. She loved to fly. Most of all, she loved to race.

Her dreamskoot was flying beautifully. The engine hummed smoothly even at the highest speeds. She had spent hours oiling the wings until they were in perfect condition. Harley proved it by cornering around a chimney so tightly, her skoot tipped right over onto its side. The wings held their shape against the wind without the slightest sign of a split or tear.

Harley knew all the tricks to squeeze every last drop of speed out of her skoot and in no time at all she was flying above her customer's street. She glanced at her speed challenge timer. The clock had stopped. She had arrived. She spotted a double-decker bus trundling down the road. "Very handy," she grinned, zooming down to land neatly on the roof.

Settling back in her saddle, she checked out the delivery address details on her screen. "Now, let's see. Jenny. Six years old. Number twenty-seven..." Harley glanced up. The houses in this street were all set well back from the road, behind high stone walls. She checked the numbers on the pillars at the bottom of each driveway. Number twenty-seven was just ahead. "My stop, I think," said Harley, taking off from the roof of the bus and zipping away up the gravelled driveway.

The house was an old Victorian mansion. "Very posh," said Harley, backing up and gazing at the front of the house. "There must be at least twenty bedrooms in this place. So where's Jenny?" She brought up a plan

of the house on her map screen. The red dot was flashing in a ground-floor room at the back of the house.

It was a lot less grand at the back. There was no garden, just a big yard with a few cars parked in it. A line of wheelie bins stood by the back door. Harley frowned. This house did not look like a family home. "Strange," she said.

"Yes, you are," said a voice right beside her.

Harley shot skywards. She was as high as the chimney tops before she looked back. There was another dreamskoot hovering beside the back door. It was battered and dirty but its engine purred with power. Its rider was not wearing a helmet and his fair hair stuck up in windblown spikes. "Dare!" Harley yelled, zipping back down into the yard with a delighted grin on her face. She pulled up beside his dreamskoot and gave him a fierce hug. "What are you doing here?"

"You mean besides scaring the pants off you?" asked Dare.

"I wasn't scared," said Harley.

"Of course you weren't." Dare's bright blue eyes sparkled.

"Shut up," said Harley, punching Dare on the arm.

"Oww!" Dare tumbled away across the yard, pretending that the punch had sent his dreamskoot into a spin. Harley smiled fondly as she watched his clowning. She and Dare went back a long way. They had lived together in the same Dreamside orphanage since they were babies. Their parents had all died in the Battle of the Gateway, bravely protecting their dream centre against an invasion of vicious sewer rats. Harley touched the tattered kerchief at her neck.

"Seriously," she said, when Dare skidded to a halt beside her once more. "What are you doing here?"

"Working," said Dare, patting the

large glass jars strapped to the side of his dreamskoot.

Dare was a Maverick. Mavericks and Collectors both gathered human emotions to supply the Dream Kitchens with raw dream ingredients, but they worked in very different ways. Collectors harvested the emotions that filtered down into their deep underground caverns. They worked beneath Earthside buildings such as hospitals, airports and football stadiums, where there were always plenty of supplies to gather. Mavericks worked above ground, tracking down unexpected outbursts of human feelings that the Collectors could not reach. They worked alone and without back-up. It was exciting, often dangerous, work, and it suited Dare perfectly. "Collectors are like boring old farmers," he would often say. "But we Mavericks are hunters!"

Harley smiled. She and Dare were very much alike. They both loved excitement. "Has the hunting been good tonight?" she asked.

Dare stopped smiling. "The hunting has been excellent," he said sadly. "My collecting jars are completely full."

"Well you don't seem very happy about it," said Harley. She frowned at his collecting jars. They looked empty but she could hear faint scratches and taps against the inside of the glass. "What have you got in there?"

"Have a look," said Dare, holding out a pair of green-tinted collecting shades.

Harley put on the shades. They were fitted with special lenses that made human feelings visible. With the shades on, she could see that the jars were full of flitting dark shadows. Some were shaped like bat wings. Others coiled like

smoke or hovered like wasps.

They all had one thing in common. Claws. It was the claws that Harley could hear scratching against the glass.

"Yuk!" she said, gazing into the jars. "What are they?"

"Terror, sadness, loneliness, loss. They all came from the same human, which makes them much more valuable. Instant nightmare mix. Very useful in a busy Dream Kitchen. I should get a lot for this catch," said Dare. But again he did not sound very happy about it.

"One human is having all these bad feelings?" Harley whispered.

Dare nodded. "A little girl. Come on. I'll show you."

Harley and Dare flew along the side of the building, heading for an open window. "How did you know those – things – would be here to collect tonight?" Harley asked.

"I didn't," said Dare. "Not for sure. I just called on the off-chance. This is a children's home, you see."

"You mean like our orphanage back home?" Harley asked.

"Yes. And, like our orphanage, it's mainly a happy place," said Dare. "But every now and then they take in a short-stay child. Someone who suddenly has nowhere else to go."

"Because something has happened to their family," Harley guessed, touching the kerchief at her neck.

"That's right. I can always fill my collecting jars when a short-stay child arrives. One was brought in earlier tonight."

"The little girl," said Harley.

Dare nodded. Together they slipped through the open window into a long, empty corridor. They rose up to the ceiling and then flew along towards the far end.

"House mother," Dare whispered, nodding at an open door. Harley peeked in and saw a female human sitting on a shabby sofa reading a book. She looked kind but tired.

They carried on to the last door in the corridor. "Here she is," Dare whispered, floating through the doorway into a small bedroom. There were two beds. One bed was empty. In the other, a little

girl was curled up under the duvet in an exhausted sleep. Her eyes were red and her face was swollen with crying. Every now and then she sobbed in her sleep.

"Poor thing," said Harley. "Do you know what happened?"

Dare nodded. "I heard the staff talking. Her mum had to go to hospital in an ambulance."

"What about the dad?"

"There isn't one," said Dare. "And the grandmother won't be here until tomorrow. She's flying back from holiday—"

"Flying?" Harley interrupted. "Really?"

"In a plane," smiled Dare.

"Oh. I knew that. What's wrong with her mum?"

"Something burst. An app… thingy."

"Appendix," said Harley, nodding her head wisely. "Humans often have to have them taken out. She'll be fine."

"Jenny doesn't know that," said Dare. "She doesn't really understand what's going on. That's why she's so upset."

"Did you say Jenny?" Harley looked at the little girl and then at the order details on her screen. "That's the name of my customer." She pulled the dream box from its padded holder and looked at the label. *"Darkest Fears,"* she read. "Oh dear. It's a nightmare. That's all she needs. What if she wakes up? She's all alone. Why isn't she upstairs with the other girls? What sort of a place is this?"

"Calm down," said Dare. "Jenny is a sleepwalker. They thought it would be safer to keep her on the ground floor. And the house mother just down the corridor is keeping an eye on her."

"Hmmm," said Harley, remembering the kind-looking human on the sofa. She looked down at the box in her hand. "Well. I suppose I'd better deliver this," she said reluctantly.

"Will you help me with something first?" Dare asked.

Harley slammed the nightmare back into her dreamskoot holder, glad of an excuse to delay the delivery. "Let's go!" she said.

Dare took her back along the corridor, past the house mother's room where the human was now dozing on the sofa. Harley followed him out into the yard and along to the wheelie bins. "See the bin closest to the back door?" Dare asked. "With that cardboard box caught under the lid?"

"Yeah."

"Have a look inside. Go on."

Harley flew up to the bin. The cardboard box had wedged the lid open. She eased through the gap. The inside of the bin was dark and smelly. Harley put her headlight onto full beam. A pair of eyes gazed up at her. Harley jumped and then looked again. The eyes were stitched onto a little cloth face. Lying among the empty tins and banana skins was a very old raggedy doll. It had been washed so many times, the dress had

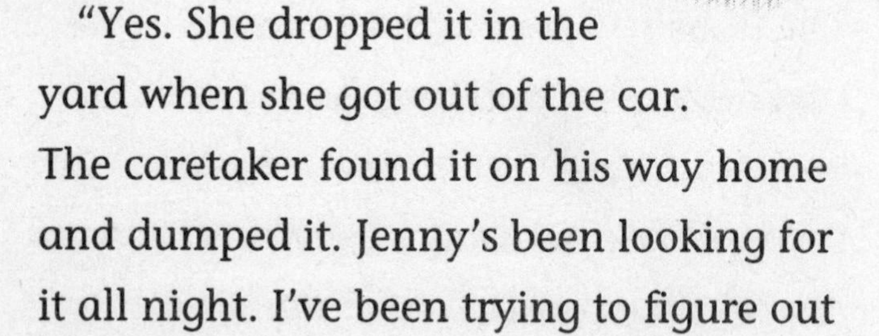

lost its colour and the woollen plaits were frayed.

"Is it Jenny's doll?" asked Harley, emerging from the bin.

"Yes. She dropped it in the yard when she got out of the car. The caretaker found it on his way home and dumped it. Jenny's been looking for it all night. I've been trying to figure out how to get it out of the bin for her."

Harley nodded. "So that's why you're still here."

Dare eased into the bin for another look. "I thought, if we each tied a plait to our saddles, we could probably lift the doll out of here and fly it down the corridor to Jenny. "What do you think?" he called.

Harley was about to reply when the back door suddenly flew open. "Human!" she hissed, diving down behind the bin.

It was too late for Dare to get out of the bin. He stayed hidden inside as the house mother stepped into the yard. Harley peered out from her hiding place. The house mother was rubbing her eyes and taking in deep breaths of the cold night air to wake herself up. She shivered and rubbed at her arms. *Good,* thought Harley. *She won't stay long.*

Harley was right. A moment later, the house mother turned to go back in. Harley began to relax, but then something dreadful happened. Just before the door closed behind her, the human noticed the cardboard box

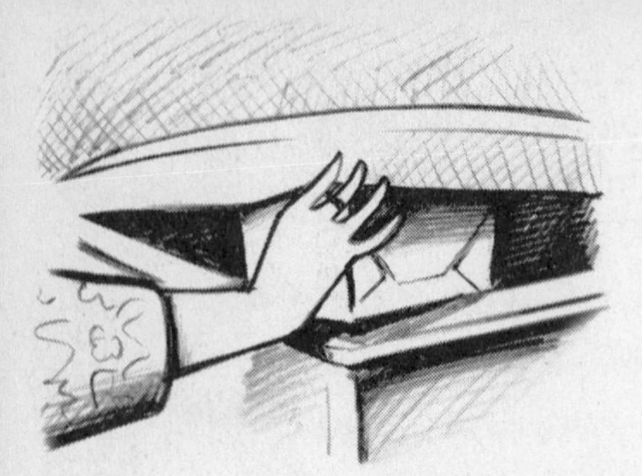

sticking out of the bin. To Harley's horror, she gave it a shove.

Thud! The box fell into the bin on top of Dare.

Slam! The heavy lid crashed into place, trapping him inside.

As soon as the back door closed behind the human, Harley zipped up to the top of the wheelie bin. "Dare? Dare, can you hear me?"

There was no answer. Harley flew around the bin in a panic. She knew she could not lift the heavy rubber lid even a millimetre. How was she going to free Dare? She

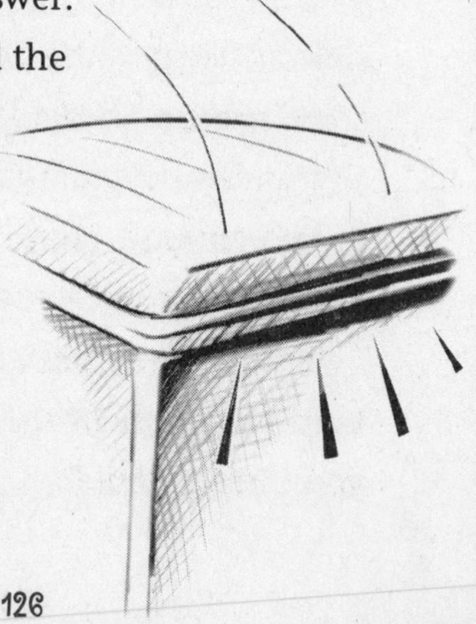

thought about calling the Dreamside Search and Rescue squad, but then shook her head. Search and Rescue would not come out for Dare. Mavericks worked outside the system. They were expected to look after themselves.

Harley kicked the side of the bin. There was no answering kick from inside. She flew back up to the lid, trying to think of some way to lift it, although she knew that really only a human would be strong enough. Harley stopped. A human! She knew just where to get one.

"Dare?" she shouted. "I'm going to get help, do you hear me? I'm going to get you out of there."

Again, there was no answer. Harley swallowed a sob and flew back to Jenny's room as fast as she could. She yanked the dream box from the holder and flew across to Jenny's bed.

She was about to try something very dangerous. The correct way to make a dream-drop was to fly in and let go of the box well before it reached the human. As soon as a dream box touched a human's skin, it would be sucked in. If a Dream Fetcher was still holding onto the box, they would be sucked in too. Dreams, especially nightmares, were very dangerous places – and most Dream Fetchers who fell into one did not survive.

Harley looked down at Jenny. "I hope you *do* sleepwalk," she whispered. Holding the dream box tightly, she flew down to Jenny and pressed it against the little girl's cheek. Everything began to spin. Harley closed her eyes as she fell into the dream. When she opened them again, she was a human girl, lying in a bed. She turned her head on the pillow. Jenny was asleep in the other bed. "So far so good," whispered Harley, climbing out of bed. She was wearing a long white nightdress and her feet were bare. She padded over to Jenny's bed.

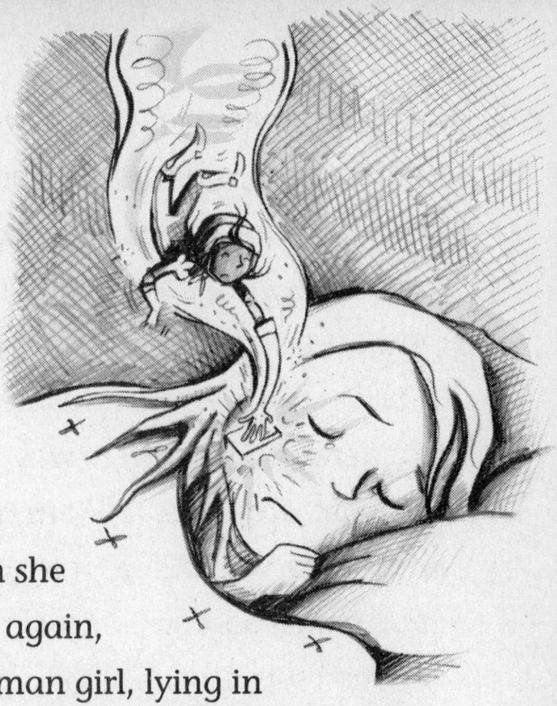

"Now all I have to do is get you along to the end of the corridor," she said, gazing down at the sleeping girl. "It can't be that hard. Can it?"

She was about to shake Jenny awake when something scratched at the window. Jenny's eyes sprang open. "Who are you?" she said.

"Hello, I'm Harley. You were asleep when I arrived. I'm staying here tonight too, in the other bed."

Jenny nodded and sat up. Her hair had been put into two plaits, just like her raggedy doll's, but one plait had unravelled in her sleep. She looked very small and very scared as she searched under her pillow and then stared around the room.

"Are you looking for your raggedy doll?" asked Harley.

Jenny nodded. Her eyes began to fill with tears.

"I know where it is," said Harley. "Come on, I'll show you."

As Jenny climbed out of bed there was another scratch at the window.

"What is that?" asked Harley.

"Wolves," said Jenny. As soon as she said it, a wolfish face appeared at the window. Then another one. Then a third. They snarled in at Jenny and Harley.

"Don't worry," said Harley. "They can't break the window. That's safety glass."

"It won't help," said Jenny. "They're nightmare wolves. They always get in."

Crack!

As soon as Jenny finished speaking, a piece of safety glass fell out of the window. The lead wolf stuck its head through the hole and snarled.

"This way," said Harley, grabbing Jenny by the wrist and pulling her out of the room. She yanked the door shut

behind them just as something slammed against the wood on the other side.

"Easy-peasy," said Harley, but her voice was shaking. She knew that everything in Jenny's nightmare was a very real danger to her. If a wolf caught Jenny, she might be terrified but she would still wake up safe in her bed afterwards. If a wolf attacked Harley, she would die.

Harley stared at the dark corridor ahead of them. The only way to free Dare from the wheelie bin was to get Jenny to open the lid. But first she had to walk through a nightmare full of Jenny's worst fears. She would have to stay very alert if she wanted to survive.

"Where's Molly?" Jenny asked.

"Is Molly the name of your raggedy doll?"

Jenny nodded. Her chin began to tremble. "My mum made her."

"Come on," said Harley. "I'll take you to Molly."

She padded down the corridor with Jenny beside her. The corridor was much darker in Jenny's nightmare than it was in real life. It was longer, too. Harley knew the back door was at the other end, but it was too far away to see. As she peered into the darkness she saw a movement.

Slap, slap, slap.

Something was walking down the corridor towards them. Jenny stopped suddenly. Harley looked at the dark shape as it approached. It had long, narrow feet that slapped down onto the floor with every step. It had frizzy hair and a pointy hat. "What is that?" whispered Harley.

"Clown," said Jenny in a scared little voice.

As soon as Jenny spoke, the clown stepped out of the shadows and Harley could see it clearly. It had a red nose and a big painted smile. *Slap, slap, slap.* It strode towards them in its silly long shoes.

"Why are you scared of clowns?" asked Harley.

Jenny did not answer. She was staring up at the clown with a look of terror on her face. The clown came closer. It seemed to be growing larger with every step. "Jenny! Why don't you like clowns?" demanded Harley. The clown was even closer now. She could see every detail of its costume. It had baggy trousers, a stripy jacket and a joke flower in its buttonhole. Its eyes were black. "Tell me, Jenny! Why are you frightened of clowns?"

The clown stretched out its white-gloved hands to grab them.

"Quick!" yelled Harley. "Tell me!"

"Their smiles aren't real," sobbed Jenny.

The clown's mouth was open. Its teeth were big and square. It bent its huge head down towards them. Harley looked at the painted smile and then at the joke flower in the clown's buttonhole. "Then let's get rid of the smile," she said, pulling open the clown's jacket. There was a green plastic bulb on the end of the flower stem. Harley squeezed the bulb. A jet of water shot out of the middle of the flower onto the clown's face. The painted smile dissolved in the water and disappeared. The clown stopped, frozen in place. Harley reached up and poked it on the nose. With a loud pop, the clown vanished.

"Easy-peasy," said Harley, grinning at Jenny. "Come on."

They ran the rest of the way down the dark corridor. The door at the end was closer now. Harley could see the outline of the wheelie bin on the other side of the glass. She ran even faster, looking from side to side. Wolves. Clowns. What would be next?

She stepped into something cold and wet. "What is that?" she asked.

"Water," said Jenny, gazing down at the puddle. "And I can't swim!"

As soon as Jenny finished speaking,

the puddle of water rose up and filled the corridor. Suddenly they were in the deep end of a swimming pool. Harley tried to swim but her long white nightdress was heavy with water. The weight was pulling her down. Beside her, Jenny was having the same problem.
"To the side," spluttered Harley.

They scrambled to the side of the pool and grabbed the handrail.

"There," gasped Harley. "We're safe now. All we have to do is work our way along to the shallow end."

"We can't," said Jenny miserably.

"Why not?"

"Because the handrail always comes away from the side."

"Don't say that!" yelled Harley, but she was too late. As soon as Jenny finished speaking, the bolts attaching the handrail to the side of the pool began to

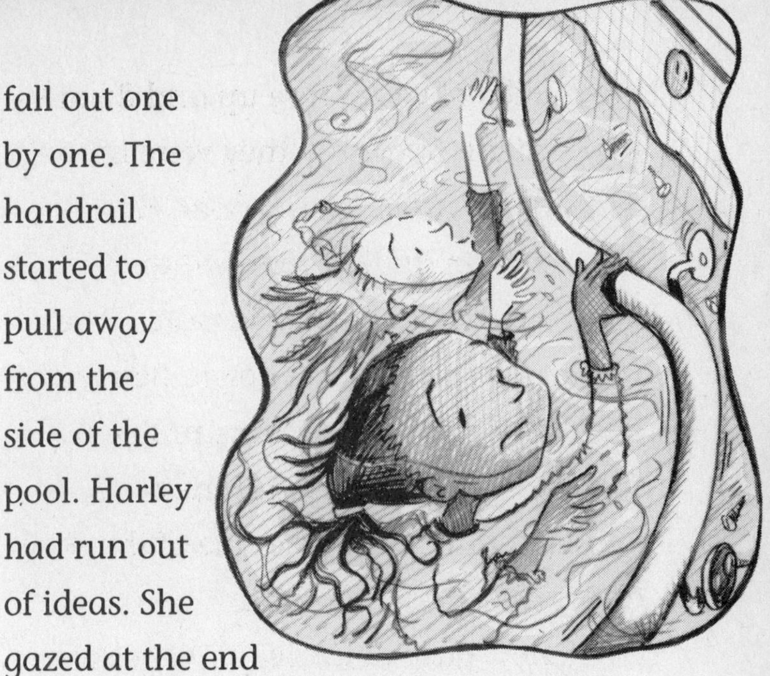

fall out one by one. The handrail started to pull away from the side of the pool. Harley had run out of ideas. She gazed at the end of the corridor. The back door was so close but she could not reach it. A whole section of the handrail came away and she sank even further into the pool.

Sorry, Dare, she thought, staring at the outline of the wheelie bin through the glass of the door. *I can't help you. I'm too busy drowning*. "Oh! Wait a minute," she gasped, suddenly remembering what else was in the bin. "Jenny, do you see that wheelie bin on the other side of the door?"

"Yes," spluttered Jenny.

"Molly's in there," coughed Harley, spitting water from her mouth.

"She is?" Jenny gasped.

"You're nearly there, Jenny," said Harley. "All you have to do is reach the door."

"But I can't swim!" wailed Jenny as another section of handrail came away from the side. "I always sink!"

As soon as Jenny finished speaking, Harley sank under the water. She struggled to the surface again. "It's *your* nightmare," she spluttered. "Change it!"

"How?"

"Whatever you say comes true. Say something, Jenny!"

Jenny looked doubtful. Harley sank again. This time it was much harder to

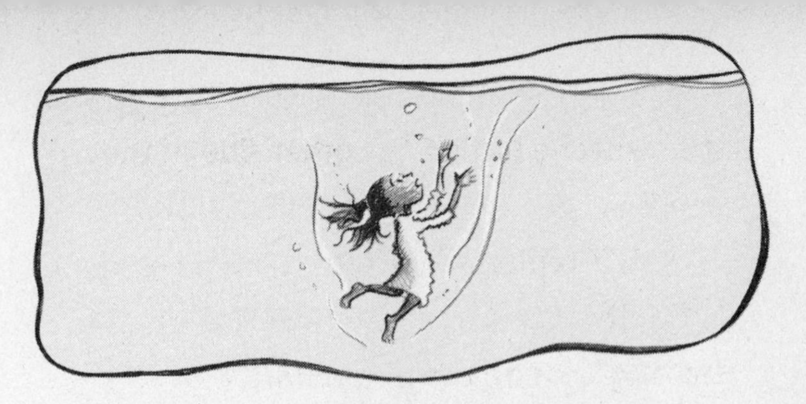

claw her way back to the surface. "Do you want to save Molly from the bin?" she gasped as soon as her mouth cleared the water.

Jenny nodded. She took a breath. "It's not a swimming pool," she said firmly. "It's a paddling pool."

As soon as she spoke, the white tiles vanished and the water drained away. They were left clinging together in the middle of a little blue plastic paddling pool.

"Easy-peasy," Harley wheezed.

Jenny splashed out of the pool, pushed through the door and ran outside. Harley followed her, coughing up water. Jenny

stood on her tiptoes at the top of the steps and grabbed the lid of the wheelie bin. She pulled the handle and the lid swung open. It hit the wall with a crash.

"Molly!" Jenny cried joyfully. She reached in, grabbed the raggedy doll and hugged it to her. Harley tried to look for Dare but suddenly the top of the bin seemed to be way above her head. The back yard began to whirl. Harley closed her eyes. When she opened them *again*, she was sitting on her dreamskoot right in

front of Jenny's huge bare foot. The nightmare was over. Jenny had woken up and Harley had made it back to Earthside.

The back door opened and the house mother walked out. Harley took off just in time to avoid being stepped on. She flew behind the bin and hid in the shadows. "Don't be frightened, dear," said the house mother, putting an arm around Jenny's shoulders. "You've been sleepwalking again. The hospital called," she added. "Your mum has had her operation and everything is fine. How about coming back to bed? It's a bit cold out here, don't you think?"

"Where's Harley?" Jenny asked.

"Harley?"

"The girl in the other bed," Jenny said. "She saved me. And Molly. I have to say thanks."

"The other bed is empty, dear," the house mother said. "You must have dreamed her. Let's go inside."

As soon as the door closed behind Jenny and the house mother, Harley flew up to the top of the bin.

"Dare?" she called, peering inside.

There was no answer. Harley's eyes filled with tears. She had survived a nightmare and brought Jenny to open the bin. Had it all been for nothing?

"Dare?" she whispered.

The cardboard box moved. A spiky-haired head emerged.

"Dare!" cried Harley. "You're OK!"

"Hardly," Dare grimaced, peeling a soggy cornflake from his trousers. "But I am very lucky. If Jenny hadn't come along, I would have been stuck."

"Luck doesn't come into it," said Harley, wrinkling her nose at the smell as Dare flew up out of the bin to join her. "I brought Jenny here."

"You did?" said Dare, giving Harley a look full of admiration. "How did you manage that?"

"Oh, it was easy!" laughed Harley, doing victory rolls all around the snowy back yard. "Easy-peasy!"

Snow Fairies

"Please Land Here."

Vert could not believe what he was seeing. The sign hung on the inside of his customer's bedroom window. It was handwritten in pink ink and framed in fairy lights. A line of arrows stretched from the sign to the bottom corner of the window. He followed the arrows. They led to a little door.

Vert stared. "OK," he muttered, poking a finger under his helmet to scratch his

head. "What's going on?"

The door in the window was just the right size for a Dream Fetcher. It was painted a glossy green. The hinges and the knob were made of polished brass. There was even a welcome mat. Vert backed away, suspecting a trap. Humans were not supposed to know about Dream Fetchers. So why did this bedroom window have a Dream Fetcher-sized door cut into it?

He checked his delivery details. "Middle cottage. Stone-built terrace. On the river bank. Under the railway bridge." It was definitely the right address. He flew back to the window and peered through the glass. His customer was a nine-year-old girl called Daisy. He could see her in the glow of the night light. She was fast asleep. She didn't look the sort to be setting traps for Dream Fetchers. He looked more closely at Daisy's night light. It was shaped like a fairy.

"Aha!" Vert said, understanding. Daisy's bedroom walls were covered with posters of fairies. There were fairies on her duvet cover and a pair of human-sized fairy wings hung from her door.

Vert nodded. The green door and the "Please Land Here" sign were not meant for him at all. Daisy was hoping a fairy might pay her a visit.

"Sorry, Daisy." Vert smiled as he pushed open the green door. "It's only me." He steered his dreamskoot inside and flew across to his sleeping customer. There was another sign stuck to the mirror above her bedside table.

Make Yourself at Home.

Vert looked at the table. Daisy had left out a matchbox bed with a cotton-wool mattress and a pink quilted cover. A chair and footstool stood next to the bed. They were carved from a champagne cork and decorated with glitter.

Vert glanced across at the sleeping girl. He hesitated. He knew he should deliver the dream and leave, but it was freezing outside and the bed and chair looked very tempting. He brought his dreamskoot in to land on the bedside table and clambered out of the saddle. It felt good to be back on solid ground. He tiptoed across to the matchbox bed and tested the mattress with his hand.

"Hmm. Not quite firm enough for me," he said. He moved across to the chair and sat down. It had been made for a fairy, not a slightly plump Dream Fetcher, but Vert found it surprisingly comfortable. The cork had been hollowed out into just the right shape for his bottom.

"Fancy that," he said, leaning back in the chair and putting his feet up. He looked down at his boots. They twinkled back at him. Vert jumped up. He was covered in sticky glitter from the chair. He sighed and plodded back to his dreamskoot, leaving little silver footprints all the way. How was he going to explain his new glittery look to Team Leader Flint? Then he remembered that the gateway filters would not let anything through from Earthside. The glitter would be sucked off his uniform as he passed through to Dreamside.

At least Daisy will be pleased, he thought, looking back at the silver footprints. *She'll think a fairy paid her a visit in the night.*

Once he was airborne again, Vert pulled Daisy's dream from his holder and let it drop onto her cheek. "Sweet dreams," he whispered as the little girl began to smile in her sleep. He flew out through the green door, landed his dreamskoot on the welcome mat and took a look at the sky. Above the town it was still clear and full of stars, but there was a bank of low cloud over the inland hills. The snow was on its way. He would have to fly fast to make it home to Dreamside.

Speed was a problem for Vert. He could fly perfectly well as long as he never looked down. Or up. Or sideways. Or anywhere at all, except at the two screens on his control panel. The map screen showed him where he had to go and the D.R.E.A.M. screen warned him of any obstacles ahead. As long as he kept his gaze fixed on the screens, he could pretend that he was not high in the air at all. But even the best navigation systems were not as good as a sharp pair of eyes. Flying blind meant flying slow.

Vert looked up at the sky again. The snow clouds had moved closer and the wind was getting stronger. He gulped. Already he felt sick and dizzy and he had not even left the windowsill.

"Get a grip!" he muttered. "You can do this!"

Vert took off and flew over the garden, staying as low as he dared. Suddenly the snowy ground rose up in front of him. He tried to swerve, but it was too late.

The next thing he knew, he was lying on his back in the snow. A huge white shape towered over him. Vert gazed up at it, trying to work out what he had crashed into. A second later, he screamed. A monster! It had a white lumpy head and a hunched back. It was glaring at him with eyes of stone.

Vert's boots scrabbled in the snow as he tried to push himself away. The monster did not move. Vert sat up. He looked at the monster more closely and then gave a shaky laugh.

"It's a snowman! No. A snow fairy," he said, realizing that the hunched back was supposed to be a pair of folded wings. He scrambled to his feet. His dreamskoot lay on its side in the snow not far away. Vert grabbed the handlebars and pulled the little machine upright. The headlight was still on and the wings were folded neatly away under the footplates. He checked them over and nodded happily. Everything was still working. He had been very lucky.

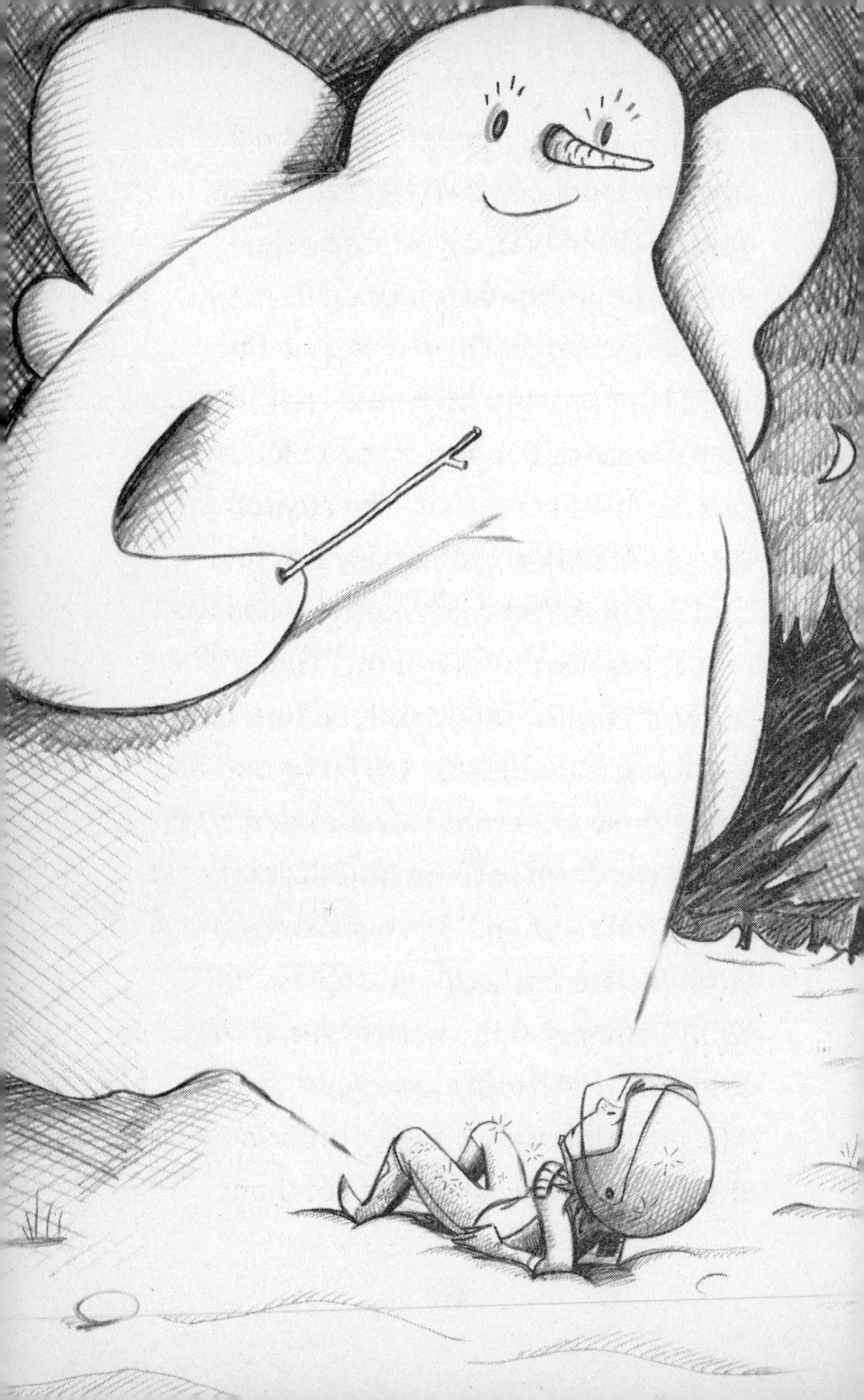

Just as he was about to climb back into the saddle, something ran across his headlight beam. Vert froze. He caught a glimpse of glittering dark eyes and sharp fangs. There it was again! It had a long, thin body and short legs. Its fur was white apart from a black tuft on the tip of its tail. The creature disappeared into the darkness. Where had it gone? Vert was too frightened to move. His heart was beating so hard he thought it must sound as loud as a drum.

The creature hissed. An answering hiss came from somewhere over to Vert's left. There were two of them and they seemed to be stalking him. Vert backed away from his dreamskoot and kept going until he reached the base of the snow fairy. He had slipped away just in time. The creatures were sniffing around his dreamskoot now. He could see them quite clearly in the headlight beam. Weasels.

Stepping as quietly as he could in the crunchy snow, Vert edged around until he was facing Daisy's snow fairy. He boosted himself up and began to climb. Behind him, one of the weasels hissed. It sounded very loud in the quiet garden. Clinging to the side of the snow fairy, Vert looked over his shoulder. The weasels were both staring straight at him.

For a heartbeat Vert and the weasels were all as still as statues.

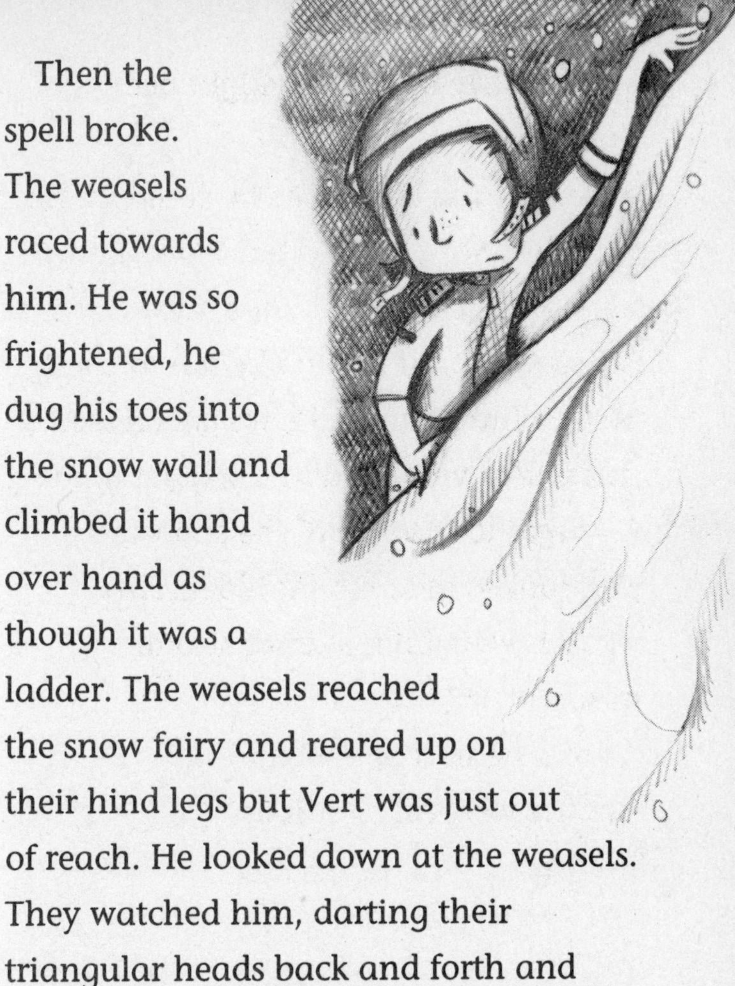

Then the spell broke. The weasels raced towards him. He was so frightened, he dug his toes into the snow wall and climbed it hand over hand as though it was a ladder. The weasels reached the snow fairy and reared up on their hind legs but Vert was just out of reach. He looked down at the weasels. They watched him, darting their triangular heads back and forth and sniffing the air with their narrow snouts.

He began to edge sideways but he had only managed to reach the edge of the snow fairy's wing when the weasels snaked across to him. With one hand he ripped off his helmet. "Go away!" he screamed, throwing it at them.

The next instant he gave a cry of despair. His dreamcom was in his helmet. He had just thrown away his only chance of calling for help.

The helmet bounced away across the snow. One weasel chased after it while the other began to climb towards him. Vert closed his eyes. He felt a shudder and then heard a hiss and a muffled thump. When he opened his eyes again, the weasel was back on the ground, shaking snow from its fur. The bottom part of the snow fairy's wing had fallen off, taking the weasel down with it.

Vert looked down at the remaining half of the wing. There was a crack in the snow just below his feet. His eyes widened. There was a chance he could still get out of this alive. He rammed his heel into the snow again and again. The crack widened until, finally, the rest of the wing broke off, leaving him balanced on a narrow ledge. Chunks of snow fell to the ground, triggering the security light. The garden lit up like a football pitch.

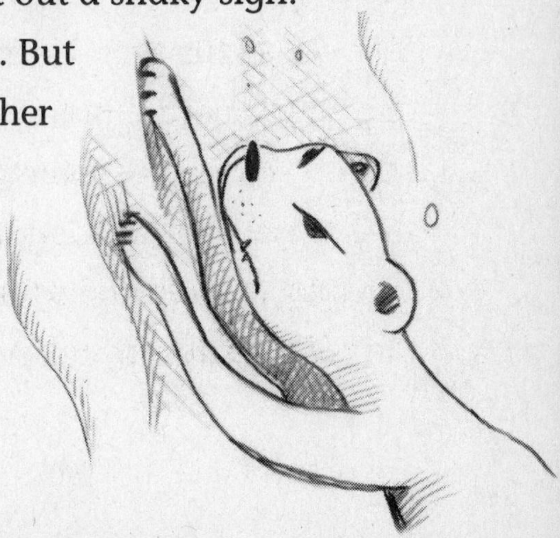

The weasels snaked away into the darkness. Vert let out a shaky sigh. He was still alive. But now he had another problem – he was trapped on a crumbling ledge of snow high above the ground. A light went on in the house. The back door opened and a human stepped out into the snow. Vert flattened himself against the snow fairy.

"What is it, Dad?" a little girl's voice called from inside.

"Nothing, Daisy. Probably just a cat or a fox," the human replied.

"What about my rabbits?"

"I'll check," said Daisy's father. "You go back to bed."

"Oh, my poor snow fairy!" said Daisy, appearing in the doorway. "The wing's fallen off."

She shoved her feet into wellington boots decorated with fairies. Vert squeaked with fright as she came through the snow towards him. He had nowhere to go. Daisy walked right up to the snow fairy. She inspected the pieces of broken wing. Then she glanced up at the place where the wing had come away.

She looked straight at Vert. Her eyes widened. She blinked and leant closer to the little snow shelf. Vert began to tremble. Daisy's face was only inches from him.

"Oh," Daisy breathed, gazing at Vert. Her warm breath washed over him, making him realize how cold he had become. He shivered, making all the glitter on his clothes sparkle.

"You're a snow fairy!" Daisy exclaimed. The warmth of her breath hit the snow ledge a second time and a large chunk fell away from one side. Vert stood as still as he could.

"I knew it," said Daisy. "I knew fairies

were real. I never stopped believing you would come to see me one day."

Another chunk of ledge fell away. Vert was left standing on a tiny square platform. Daisy held out her hand, palm up. Vert did the only thing he could. He stepped onto Daisy's fingers and walked down into her palm.

A smile of pure delight spread across Daisy's face. "My name is Daisy," she said. "What's yours?"

Vert was trembling but he pulled himself together and began to play his part. Putting one hand behind his back he made a courtly bow. "Greetings, Daisy," he shouted. "My name is ..." He hesitated. "Vert" did not sound very fairy-like. "Um ... my name is Twinkle Frost."

"Can you fly?" Daisy asked, studying Vert for any sign of wings.

"Of course I can," Vert yelled. "Put me down and I'll show you."

Daisy nodded and lowered her hand to the ground. Vert felt as though he was in an out-of-control elevator. He grabbed onto Daisy's thumb to steady himself. His stomach lurched. He swallowed hard. It would not help at all to be sick onto Daisy's hand.

Daisy laid her hand flat against the snow and Vert slid off onto the ground. Daisy looked at him expectantly. Vert made another bow and backed towards his dreamskoot.

"Daisy! What are you doing down there?"

"There's a snow fairy!" Daisy cried, turning to look at her father.

Vert turned and scrambled away through the snow. He found his helmet. Grabbed it. Jammed it onto his head.

"Come inside," Daisy's father called. "It'll still be there in the morning."

Vert sprinted for his dreamskoot and yanked it out of the snow.

"No, not *my* snow fairy," Daisy said, still looking towards the house. "This is a real one! He's called Twinkle Frost!"

Vert winced as he scrambled into the saddle. *Twinkle Frost...?*

"Very nice. Now inside. Quickly."

"Come and see him, Dad!" Daisy called.

"Lift off," said Vert hastily. His

dreamskoot rose into the air. Vert breathed a sigh of relief. Everything was working.

"Daisy. I'm waiting..."

"But Dad..."

"Wings out," Vert ordered. The wings opened out from under the footplates. They shone with a silvery glow in the glare from the security light.

"Daisy! Inside. Now. It's starting to snow."

Daisy turned back to Vert and gave a gasp of wonder as she saw him hovering in the air above her head. All she could see was his headlight and the silvery wings of his dreamskoot. "Oh, Twinkle Frost!" she cried, scrambling to her feet. "You can fly! You look lovely!"

Vert dipped his headlight at Daisy, turned his dreamskoot and shot off down the garden.

"Bye, Twinkle Frost!" called Daisy as she ran back to the house.

Vert flew to the river bank and landed on top of a high stone wall. He was breathing so hard and fast he thought he might pass out.

Splat!

A large snowflake landed on the stone beside him. Vert jumped.

Splat! Splat! Splat!

Three more snowflakes hit the stone and more were falling all around him. Vert groaned. He did not know if he could make it home. He had run out of courage and he felt very alone. A tear trickled down his cheek as he looked up into the Earthside sky. The snow was falling more thickly now. Two snowflakes caught his eye. They were flying across the sky instead of falling straight down. They were heading straight for him!

Vert was about to scream when he realized that the two snowflakes had headlights. His scream turned into a shout of joy. It was Midge and Harley! They brought their dreamskoots in to land on the wall beside him.

"I'm so glad to see you!" said Vert. "I thought I was on my own."

"You're never on your own, Vert," said Midge. "We're the Dream Team, remember?"

"But how did you know I was in trouble?"

"I was watching everyone's helmet icons on my return flight," said Midge. "I saw you leave your delivery address and then just stop dead. When you didn't move for ages, I called up Harley and Snaffle."

"Is Snaffle here too?" Vert asked, looking around.

"No," Harley growled as she took off her helmet. "We were neck and neck, racing for the gateway, when Midge called us on the dreamcom. She said you needed help so I turned around right away. When I looked back, Snaffle was still heading for the gateway." Harley scowled. "I would've won," she said.

"Of course you would have," said Midge. "Come on," she added as another large snowflake landed right beside her dreamskoot. "We need to get back."

"I don't think I can do it," said Vert in a wobbly voice. The shock was setting in. His ears were drooping badly and he was shivering.

"You don't need to," Midge smiled. "We'll merge our N.A.P.s."

"And you can just sit back and let us navigate," Harley added.

"Thanks," Vert sighed.

They lined up side by side and all pressed the red buttons on their control panels. Instantly, their Neutral Atmosphere Providers sprang into action, forming one big bubble around all three dreamskoots.

"Twinkle Frost?" said Harley as they rose into the air. "Did I hear that human call you Twinkle Frost?"

Vert blushed. "It's a long story," he said.

"Well, we've got a long trip home," said Midge.

So, as they settled in their saddles and drifted back to Dreamside protected inside their warm, bright N.A.P. bubble, Vert told them the story of Daisy and the snow fairy.

They were still laughing about it as they passed through the gateway and brought their dreamskoots in to land. Team Leader Flint strode towards them as they gathered on the metal walkway. The look on her face stopped them in mid-giggle.

"So!" snapped Team Leader Flint. "You finally decided to join us. Snaffle has been back for ages! Did you forget you were supposed to be taking part in a speed challenge?"

"Sorry," Midge muttered. "We got lost."

Snaffle was standing behind Team Leader Flint. Midge gazed at him pleadingly, begging him not to say anything. Snaffle made a face but kept quiet.

"I see," Team Leader Flint sighed. "You all got lost at the same time and you all somehow ended up in exactly the same place."

"Yes, boss," whispered Midge. Vert and Harley nodded in agreement. Team Leader Flint glared at them for the longest time.

"Very well," she decided. "You are all in joint bottom place. Snaffle wins the speed challenge. He is now in the lead on the points board."

Vert, Midge and Harley all breathed a sigh of relief. For some reason, Team Leader Flint was letting them off the hook.

"Dismissed," Team Leader Flint snarled.

The three of them saluted and walked away from the launch pads. Snaffle scowled across at them, waiting for them to tease him about his shrunken uniform. But they didn't. They simply smiled at him politely.

"Congratulations, Snaffle," said Harley stiffly. "You won the speed challenge."

"Yes, congratulations," said Midge, trying not to stare at the split in the seat of his trousers.

"Well done," said Vert, turning his gaze away from Snaffle's bare belly.

They nodded politely and walked off towards the Mess Hall arm in arm.

Snaffle watched them go. Suddenly he wished they *had* teased him about his uniform. At least they would have been treating him as one of the group. He felt